The water was very cold. It was a shock. David and Tim began to swim down, angling their bodies. There was no feeling of weight, they moved through space unemcumbered. Into the dark beyond.

David had trouble knowing which way was up and which was down. They angled up a bit until the ground disappeared.

The farther they went, the more depth the dark had, not only by the absence of light so much as the quantity of dark that separated them from the lighted dome. Entropy made palpable.

Particularly paranoid this morning, he thought. It was the dark, the dark always bothered him.

Just because you're paranoid doesn't mean that they aren't really out to get you. If he lost Tim he would turn around and try to head back for the dome but there was a good chance he would miss it in the darkness. He would die of exposure in a couple of hours.

Abruptly he realized he had been moving for the space of half a dozen kicks in the direction Tim had vanished. Was he paranoid if he was correct? He turned in a full circle to see if he could catch sight of Tim, but he had gone, no way to even guess direction.

David was lost in the night.

Then his headlamp went off.

Instantly, the black rushed in at him.

Half the
Day Is Night

Maureen F. McHugh

A TOM DOHERTY ASSOCIATES BOOK
NEW YORK

This is a work of fiction. All the characters and events portrayed in this book are fictional, and any resemblance to real people or incidents is purely coincidental.

HALF THE DAY IS NIGHT

Copyright © 1994 by Maureen F. McHugh

Cover art by Paul Lehr

A Tor Book
Published by Tom Doherty Associates, Inc.
175 Fifth Avenue
New York, N.Y. 10010

Tor Books on the World-Wide Web:
http://www.tor.com

Tor® is a registered trademark of Tom Doherty Associates, Inc.

ISBN: 0-812-52410-1
Library of Congress Catalog Card Number: 94-21745

First edition: October 1994
First mass market edition: January 1996

Printed in the United States of America

0 9 8 7 6 5 4 3 2 1

This book is for four women:
Ama Selu, Arla, Evelyn and Pat.
And they all know why.

ACKNOWLEDGMENTS

Thanks to the following people: Bob Yeager, who tirelessly hounded me on technical details; all errors are mine, not his. Patrick Nielsen Hayden, who gave me time and encouragement as well as cogent suggestions. Tim Ryan and Sean Barton (Information Services-R-Us); Tim for technical assistance and Sean for being my favorite fan.

1

Underwater

The man in the reflection didn't have any eyes.

It was a trick of the lighting. He was looking into a window, out into the dark, and anywhere there was a shadow on his face the glass reflected nothing back. Holes for eyes. David looked up, the light fell on his face and his eyes appeared, he looked back out into the darkness and they became empty again.

Outside was ocean. This far below the surface it was always night. You really didn't have to go very far underwater before all the sunlight was absorbed. He should have realized but he had been unconsciously expecting Caribbean warmth, Caribbean sun, not this huge expanse of black. He shuddered, and picked up his bag and limped on, keeping his eyes away from the window. He could still see his reflection walking with him, a stride and a quick step, bobbing along, favoring his stiff knee. He followed signs directing him to Baggage Claim, they were all in English. That was a disappointment, he had hoped that there might be more French, because of the Haitian population in Caribe. They would be in Creole anyway, and he didn't know Creole.

He came through a security checkpoint and presented his passport and visa to the boy in uniform. The boy was a black with a long narrow face. So young, these soldiers. Like children dangling guns from their fingers. He was getting older, he thought, soldiers had not seemed so young when he was in the *militaire*. Thirty-three was not so old. He put his duffel on the belt through the security machine; a sign said that any comments or jokes would be treated with utmost seriousness. The boy studied his passport, then looked up at him, carefully comparing the im point by point. He remembered the points: eyes, chin, nose, hairline, eyebrows.

"Immigration is to your left," the boy said in a high, helium voice, "Welcome to Caribe." A cartoon voice from a soldier with a rifle.

It smelled like wet concrete and ammonia. The Port Authority was like a second rate airport: full of soldiers and pre-form furniture in bright grimy orange and aqua. A third world country underwater. He had not realized that it would be so dark.

He waited in line to get his suitcase, waited in line again to have his passport and visa scanned for authenticity by Immigration. He was very tired, it had been a long trip and his knee was stiff from sitting so long.

Finally, he was through Immigration and allowed out into the lobby. There was a crowd of people as he came out of Immigration, families waiting, leaning over the railing. His prospective employer was a woman, a banker named Mayla Ling. He didn't have an im. He straightened his stride trying not to limp.

A big tall blond man in a sweater and tights was holding a sign that said "DAI." He looked irritated.

"You are from Ms. Ling?" David said, hating the way he sounded.

"Yeah," the big man squeaked. "Jean David Dai?"

He nodded. His own voice sounded foolish enough, but a helium voice coming out of this big man was ludicrous. The big man said "Jeen DAY-vid," the way they did in the States, not "Jahn Dah-VEED." "Just David," he said, pronouncing it the way the other had. "I do not go by Jean."

"Tim Bennet," the big man said and offered his hand. David took it and Bennet made it into a contest of strength. He won and claimed David's big suitcase. David followed him with his duffel bag.

It was cold and everything seemed far away. It was not a trick of tiredness, he thought, it was the air mixture that made everything sound so distant. People around him were dressed in winter clothes; men in sweaters and girls in bright shiny blues and golds. This city was under the Caribbean ocean, they could make the temperature anything they wanted, why make it so cold? Did he have any long-sleeved shirts?

He followed Tim Bennet through the Port, hurrying to keep up. They went down an escalator and he studied the expanse of back. Was Bennet a bodyguard/driver? Was there more than one? He looked like he could be security but David had been told that the job was a formality, for insurance reasons. Like the job he'd had at the Caribbean Consulate when he was at University, watching monitors at night, walking through the empty building while the building system switched lights on in front of him, off behind him.

The second escalator dumped them into a concrete parking garage and again he had to hurry to keep up with Tim Bennet. The car was a tiny little black thing with a sheen iridescing blue and red under the fluorescents like oil. A little toy. Julia, the city, wasn't very big, until he had read the job description for this job and seen that it asked for a driver, he had thought they didn't use cars. Cars made no sense, burning petrochemicals in a closed system.

His one suitcase filled the trunk. What would they have done if he had two, he wondered, had them sent?

"Thisis th' karyewl b' dryvin."

He had thought his English was pretty good, but he was tired and he hadn't been listening and helium in the air mix made voices sound so strange. "Pardon me?" he said.

"This car," Bennet pointed at the little car, "this is Mayla's car. You know how to drive a car?"

"I have driven . . ." his mind went blank, he couldn't think of the word, "not a car, you know, in the *militaire*, they use them."

"Troop transports?"

David shook his head. "In French we say 'jeep'."

"Yeah, jeeps, that's what we call them. Cars probably aren't too different."

He watched Bennet clamber into the car and got in his side. He almost felt as if he was sitting on the ground, it was so low. Jeeps weren't like that. Clutch, accelerator, gear shift, brake: it all looked familiar. The instrument panel was different.

Bennet put the car in reverse and squealed away from the wall, shoved into gear and squealed again, then braked into a ramp that spiraled down. He acted as if he were angry. They came off the ramp, accelerated, Bennet leaned forward and flicked something on the keyboard on the panel, then took a box off the dash and started to rummage through it. The car continued to accelerate and Bennet was not watching. They went right into a tunnel that narrowed sharply and David grabbed the dash, the wall was centimeters from the passenger door—the car eased into a bigger tunnel. A four-lane highway in a tunnel, with lots of buses and a few cars.

"Audomadick guy danse," Bennet squeaked, still looking through the box.

He thought about the words until they made sense: "automatic guidance."

"They don't allow manual driving on the belt," Bennet

said. This time David was listening carefully and he understood. "Takes a bit of getting used to." Bennet smiled at him, pleased with himself. "Mind if I play some music?"

He shook his head. The wall of the tunnel was still close to the passenger door and then the car changed lanes smoothly as another car came out of an entrance tunnel. It made him uncomfortable. He closed his eyes but opened them again because not being able to see was worse than seeing. Bennet dropped a chip in the player. There was a moment of silence, the open sound before a song started, and then a crack of thunder and the soft patter of rain. Ambient music. The singer started; a woman's voice, distant, howling wolf-like, then coming close to sing the first line, "When I was six my father died."

"How d'ya like it?"

He shrugged. "It is okay." He didn't mind ambient music, but he didn't recognize the song. He had the feeling Bennet wanted him to dislike it. "Do you work for Ms. Ling?" he asked.

"Yeah," Bennet said.

"What do you do?" David asked.

"Your job," Bennet said grimly, or at least as grimly as anyone could in a helium falsetto.

The sub had come in at three in the afternoon but that was ten at home in Paris and he had started with a 5:12 a.m. flight from Orly. His employer was at work. He followed Bennet up the steps from the garage into a *house*. Well, he had known she was rich; she could afford to fly him from France and she could afford a car. Maybe houses were common here the way they were in the U.S. But he didn't think so.

The living room was huge, and the first thing he saw across the furniture and hardwood floor was the expanse of window. Outside was a strip of white gravel with dead coral pieces like bushes and then black ocean. Out in the ocean was another glow like a bowl turned upside down (the neighbors) but mostly just blackness.

He didn't like it, it made him feel even colder than he was. Nothing. It didn't even look like water out there, it just looked like nothing. Who would have a view on nothing? What would be the point? He looked away, looked around, tried to take in what he saw. Lots of wood, very expensive. On the white stucco wall behind him was painted a sun with a benevolent face, sleepy eyes, full pouting lips and flames like hair. It looked back at that awful view and he did, too, drawn inexorably.

Deep and black, empty, like the space between stars. He did not even get a sense of the awful pressure that must be bearing down on this building—he realized abruptly that it was a dome, built to distribute the pressure and that was the reason for the strange curve of the glass, but that didn't seem important. He couldn't take this job, he couldn't live in this place.

"Quite a view," Bennet said. "Something that makes you know you're alive."

Know you are alive? It made him think of the absurdity of his being alive.

Bennet showed him a little flat—bedroom, sitting room and little kitchen, all as impersonal as a hotel room—and he stretched out on the bed to wait. He jerked awake when he heard voices and checked his chron. It was almost six. His head was full of anxious travel dreams and he was cold. A woman's voice he thought, and ran his fingers through his hair. His boss.

She was younger than he'd expected. He thought she was in her thirties. Ling sounded like a Chinese name but she didn't look particularly Asian, she seemed American. She had black hair cut in a helmet, it swung slightly as she turned her head. She was as tall as he was, which, he had to admit, was not so very tall. She held out her hand, "Jean David Dai?" she said, pronouncing it as Bennet had.

"Just David," he said.

"Are you Chinese?" she asked.

"No, ma'am," he said, "my great-grandparents were from Viet Nam."

She nodded, "My greats," she waved her hand to indicate a couple of more greats, "were Chinese. My grandfather is Chinese-American, but I'm a, I guess I'm a mongrel." She laughed. "There aren't many Asians in Caribe. Some Cuban-Chinese, so you can get good Chinese food, and good Cuban beans and rice in the same restaurant."

She talked fast, mostly about the ninety-day probation period, because, she said, although his qualifications were fine they had no idea how comfortable they might be with each other. Tim slouched in the background, brooding.

"It's an American insurance company," she said, "and there are all sorts of restrictions about who I should hire. There's a lower premium for someone with security or military experience. They don't consider our military real military experience. Here, we don't fight much except each other, and people who join the military tend to stay in, you know?"

He nodded although he didn't know and didn't care. He was working hard to understand what she was saying.

"Can you drive?" she asked. He told her about his experience with jeeps. "In Africa," she said. "You were an officer?"

"Because I had a degree from the university," he said. "I was a lieutenant."

"Well," she said, "you'll be a driver but you're not expected to clean or cook. I have someone come in once a week and do the cleaning." She paused. He was tired of sorting things out, tired of foreignness. "It znat really nezesaribu can you youza recike?"

He didn't understand.

"A recyc," she said, slower. "For swimming, can you swim?"

"I have swim, swam, in a pool. Not like in the ocean."

"Tim can teach you tomorrow, it's not hard. And he'll help you with driving. Tim will be with us for a while longer, until everything is settled," she said.

"Ah," he said.

Tim had his hands in fists on the back of her chair, now he leaned against the chair as if doing push-ups. He didn't say anything. She did not look at him, either. Very angry, this room.

"I don't expect problems," she said, "you shouldn't either. Sometimes Tim and I eat dinner together when I'm home," Ms. Ling said. "Tonight you should eat with us, until you get some groceries."

"Thank you," he said, not feeling especially thankful at all.

He expected that the first thing he would learn was driving. The job description had specifically mentioned driving. At dinner he admitted that he was surprised that there were cars. "It seems, it would be bad for the air?" he said.

"There aren't really that many of them," Mayla said. "The people who have them live where the air recirculation is good, anyway, like here, where the system can handle it."

"But there is the highway."

Mayla frowned. "The highway?"

"The beltway," Tim said.

"Oh right," she said. "I'm sorry. I guess it is a highway, I just never thought about it. That was built when I was a girl, by President Bustamante."

"With money advanced from the World Fund. It was supposed to improve infrastructure," Tim explained.

"Roads are infrastructure," Mayla said.

"Sewers are infrastructure. Air recirculation is infrastructure," Tim said.

"I'm not disagreeing with you," Mayla said. "Everybody knows it was a misuse of the money. I just get tired of hearing you bash the government."

"Kids on the lower levels don't develop right because there isn't enough O_2 in their air mix and the bloody President for Life wants to build a highway," Tim said.

"We get the point, Tim, you don't care for the local politics," Mayla said.

"Don't get sanctimonious," Tim said. "You bitch, too."

Mayla turned to David, "It's really probably better that you didn't talk about politics, much. Here it can get you into trouble." She looked over at Tim. "Even if you carry a foreign passport."

"Aren't we prissy this evening," Tim said.

"I guess we are," Mayla said.

David looked at his fish and wished he could go to bed.

The next morning he had his lesson with the recyc system. Bennet took Ms. Ling to work and came back with a rented diving suit. It was blue with yellow reflective stripes like racing stripes down the legs and across the flippers. "I guessed the size," Bennet said. "It'll be a short lesson so it should be all right."

He took the suit back to his rooms and put it on. The tunic part was all right, but the tights were too long and they bunched around his knees and ankles. He stood in front of the mirror and tried to decide if his bad knee was obvious. It wasn't like his good one, up above it the yellow stripe down the tights showed the kind of hollow place where it was all scarred up. And he had skinny legs, legs like a chicken.

David had trouble with the seals, it took him awhile to figure out how they worked. He pulled up the hood and decided he didn't like the way he looked so he pulled it back down. He would have liked to pull his hair back, maybe he should get it cut? Long hair was old-fashioned. Eh, not the time to think about it.

He picked up his flippers and gloves and went out through the living room to a kind of utility room.

Bennet didn't have his hood up, either. He was doing something with the recyc units. David waited a moment, not sure if Bennet knew he was there or not. "I should, ah, learn what you are doing?"

Bennet started a little but didn't look up. "Yeah, the masks are in the closet."

The two masks were hanging on the wall like faces. Above them on the shelf was an AP15 rifle. He looked at the rifle. "Why does Ms. Ling have an AP15?" he asked. He could not stop himself from picking it up.

"She has a permit. I took some security classes, they said she was allowed to have one. She's going to sell it back."

David popped the clip and cracked it to see if it was clean. The clip was full, the rifle looked as if it had never been used. "I thought they did not allow them in Caribe."

"Military issue. They're not a good idea in a dome. Crack the dome, you break the integrity and the water pressure squashes the place flat."

His head was a little clearer this morning, he had followed that. "What's the range underwater?"

"I don't know," Tim sounded irritated. "You ever used one before?"

"Not underwater. In Africa." In Namibia, Windhouk, Gobabis, and the Kalahari, David thought. Before that in Serowe, Soweto, Pretoria. Mbabane and bloody Durban. *South* Africa.

"Are you going to stand there and play with the gun or are you going to hand me a mask."

"Excuse me," David said, embarrassed. But he pulled the clip before he put the rifle back and picked up two masks. Idiot. He had promised himself he would be careful, he would make a good impression on these people. It was time to forget Africa. He should have ignored the rifle. So clean, still steel blue and smelling faintly of oil.

He'd had an AP15 but not one like this with its fake

wood stock. His stock had been a metal frame with a place on it where he'd scraped it on the sidewalk in Joburg.

He could not keep this job. Too many things were not right. He had come here to start new but security was guns and fear and he did not want any of that.

"Mayla has three recyc units but the Honeywell is so old that it doesn't even have a humidifier." Bennet showed him how to put one on, how to jack the connections into the mask and hook the airfeed into the jaw. "Ever use a full facemask before?"

"Yes, and a mike. What is the setting?" He had never used one for swimming but the facemask was similar to the respirator mask they used to drill for gas attacks. He would not mention that.

"Three. Four through eight are commercial bands. Nine is official, Port Authority mostly. Most of the fish jocks use eleven and twelve, so if you need help, try those."

"Fish jocks?" David said.

"Fish jockeys. The guys that work at the fish farms. Divers. Public starts at thirteen so everything above that is crowded. Eighteen is emergency but the local police force is not very useful." Tim pulled on his flippers. "Ever swam in the dark?" Tim asked.

"No." And did not plan to do it often, thank you.

"Okay. There's a lamp mounted on your mask. The switch is a touch plate, you have to tap it twice to turn it off." He tapped once underneath the eye of the light and it came on. He tapped twice and nothing happened. Tapped twice with more emphasis and the lamp went off. "They turn on easier than they turn off."

David pulled on the mask, it was cold against his chin and smelled of metal. He tapped blindly since the lamp was on the forehead of the mask and it came on. It took him a couple of tries to get it off. Why would anyone ever want to turn one off?

"Look," Tim said, looking at the floor, "I ah, I noticed your limp. Your, ah, leg. Will it bother you swimming?"

"No," David said. "It's fine." He looked at Tim so that Tim could not look at his knee and Tim hauled the recycs out of the pool instead.

"Yeah. Ah, well then," Tim said. "As soon as we're suited up, that's it. The thing to remember when you're diving is to breathe normally. There's a telltale on your facemask that measures the amount of carbon dioxide in your blood. Just try to keep it within normal range and if you find you're having a problem, let me know."

They hauled on the recyc units, heavy with water, and David fell backward into the entry pool, copying Tim.

The water was very cold. It was a shock. The tights and suit had been uncomfortably warm but they weren't now. The pool was really a tunnel, a u-shape that dove under the ground and back up into the sea. It was about two meters across and that didn't seem like much. Tim hit an orange circle between two lights and the opening above them constricted shut. The air from the recyc had the faintest taste of the inflow valve, a rubbery taste, but it was warm. He tried drawing deep breaths to keep himself warm. The warm air in his lungs would warm his blood and that would warm all of him, but he might hyperventilate.

"When you come out," Tim's voice came clearly, "don't look straight into the lights, okay?"

"Okay." The telltale displayed amber numbers, they seemed to hang in the water in front of him about level with his left eyebrow.

They began to swim down, angling their bodies. Tim kicked lazily, David felt the water resisting his kicks. Cold, viscous saltwater. (He knew cold water did not resist any more than warm water did.) He was not sure if he was breathing properly, he seemed to be taking unnecessarily deep breaths. The telltale flickered, "26, 27, 26, 27, 28, 29, 28. . . ." What was normal and correct? Ahead was the black eye of the ocean, or was it black because the ocean had no eyes? His indicator told him his respiration was still increasing. They followed the tunnel up, no more than six meters all told, and rose out of the garden, outside the dome. They came up past the window, looking in the living room, and the benevolent sun on the wall watched them sadly.

They rose over the second floor, all dark, and their headlamps reflected off the dome. Their masks were blanks of copper in the reflection, like new smooth coins. Down the other side towards the lighted ring of garden. It would be better in the garden, in the light he would not feel so adrift.

There was no feeling of weight, they moved through space unencumbered, down past the curtained main floor to the rock garden below, where frightened fish fled silver around the dome.

Into the dark beyond. David slowed up, Tim kicked easily, moving like a shark. David followed. Light was swallowed up by ocean. He had to swim hard to catch up. He had trouble knowing which way was up and which was down. His legs were shorter, he kicked more often than Tim, and because of his bad knee he kept veering to the left. He wasn't in very good shape, but at least he wasn't worried about hyperventilating anymore.

He wished Bennet would slow down, but he wasn't about to ask for any favors. Where the hell were they going? If he lost Bennet he wouldn't have any idea where he was, although he figured he could always double back. He glanced back, he could still see the dome. But then he had to work to catch up. Funny there weren't any other domes out this way, Bennet must be taking him out away from the city. They angled up a bit until the ground disappeared. He looked back again, barely able to make out the glow of the dome. Goddamn it was cold. He should stop right here and not go any farther. He should swim back.

Which was ridiculous, Bennet must have a reason for swimming this way. He concentrated on working his bad leg better, making his kicks more even. This would be good exercise. The therapist had told him that swimming was good, no weight on his knee. No dome visible behind them. The farther they went, the more depth the dark had, not by the absence of light so much as the quantity of dark that separated them from the lighted dome. Entropy made palpable. Entropy, quit thinking like a physics student. Besides, entropy isn't a substance, it's an absence. Disorder, not malevolent, but the slow seepage of energy, the heat leaving his body, swimming slower and slower, as Bennet, the machine, would disappear into the dark at the edge of the light cast by his mask. He would be lost out here, without even directions like up and down. He wouldn't even realize he was slowing down, but he would get slower and slower until he was empty and the heat of his body evenly, randomly dispersed among the cold water.

Particularly paranoid this morning, he thought. It was the dark, the dark always bothered him. A child's distress, maman don't turn out the light.

He was panting with the effort to keep up. Bennet wanted him to ask to slow down. Macho nonsense. So ask to slow down, you stubborn fool. Where were the other domes? What were they doing out here? How did Bennet know where they were? They could be angling up. That was dangerous, could lead to the bends. Nitrogen bubbles in the blood. Stroke.

Paranoia, he sang to himself, par-a-noi-ah. Just because you're paranoid doesn't mean that they aren't really out to get you. If he lost Bennet he would turn around and try to head back for the dome but there was a good chance he would miss it in the darkness, particularly with his tendency to veer. His recyc unit would go on taking oxygen out of the water for days, but already the cold was making his hands stiff. How long until hypothermia? He would die of exposure in a couple of hours. Very convenient for Bennet. He could say he'd thought David was behind him, and he didn't know when they'd gotten separated. In a few hours, would he find another dome?

Bennet stopped suddenly, with a graceful swirl of hands

and arms, and hung. "Don't go swimming alone," he said, "It's easy to get lost."

"Paranoia," sang in David's head. "How do you know where to go?"

"I used to be a fish jockey, I've got an implant in the back of my head that tells me what direction Port Authority is. You can get one if you really want to, but you don't need it unless you plan to do a lot of swimming."

"Which way is the dome?"

Bennet pointed slightly to the right of the way David thought they had come. He peered into the dark but all he could see was the cone of light from their headlamps. Bennet's headlamp went out on his right, and as he turned, the Australian made a couple of strong kicks that took him out of the cone of David's light.

Abruptly he realized he had been moving for the space of half-a-dozen kicks in the direction Bennet had vanished. He didn't remember moving. No sign of the reflecting bands on Bennet's recyc unit, and he should have been able to see them. He halted. Was he paranoid if he was correct? He turned in a full circle to see if he caught the glint of silver off Bennet's fins or unit. Bennet could go anywhere, up or down as well as any direction. Turning had been a big mistake, without anything to orient, he wasn't sure how far he had turned or what direction Bennet had gone, what direction was the dome, from here no way to even guess direction, he was fucking well lost in the night and the amber lights of the indicator were flickering as his respiration went up; slow down, slow down, slow down. Think. He could turn off his headlamp. With his off he would stand a better chance of catching sight of Bennet's light—if Bennet's was still on. With his on he was visible to Bennet. He reached up and tapped his headlamp twice, had to do it a couple of times. His light finally went off.

Instantly, the black rushed in at him. He saw movement in the nothing, things, shapes, shells, bullets, streams coming at him, his mind making something out of the absence of sensory information, son of a bitch, he couldn't handle the dark, even if it made good sense he couldn't do it, the amber letters of the telltale going up and up, his respiration climbing, he fumbled for the lamp, cold fingers missing the plate while the only light, the amber letters of the telltale told him he was approaching hyperventilation, he used both hands and the light came on and shapes swirled only at the periphery of his vision. Panic, frigging anxiety attack, come on, he thought, be calm, you can die if you aren't calm. He whirled again, circling to find someone, nothing, but hanging there in the water his headlamp was a beacon, he was vulnerable, a still target, he had to think, think think think, think about the dark. Don't think about the dark. What would orient him? Nothing around but water, 250 meters of water between him and the sun above, below, below there was ground. Bottom. Under water ground was called bottom, swim down, folding in the water, not sure if this direction was really down but it must have been because almost instantly he saw sand and rock. The indicator said his breathing was down a little. He touched bottom, solid bottom, hard and rocky, not much sand, like the Kalahari which really had very little sand at all, groped and found a rock as big as his fist, hefted it, feeling how heavy it was, how slow he would move it in the water.

A headlamp came on close by and he turned to face it, his rock held ready, slightly behind his body, because he'd have to get real close to Bennet to use it. Bennet said matter-of-factly inside his mask, "That's exactly what you should do if you're ever lost, head for bottom."

David held the rock, waited for the other to come closer, he would be slower in the water, he would have to wait until the other was very very close. And he did not know if Bennet was armed.

"Around here you can always switch to band eleven," Tim said. "Somebody will be on the band, around here there's always someone. Of course, I was close. Sorry about that, but that's the way I was taught, you don't forget a lesson like that. You ready to go home?"

David nodded.

He dropped the rock about halfway back. Later he realized that if he'd brained Tim he'd never have been able to find his way anyway.

2

Funeral Games

Mayla did not read about Danny Tumipamba's murder in the paper because that morning she didn't get a chance to finish it.

Most mornings Mayla got into the kitchen before Tim. She made her coffee and listened for signs that he was awake. She hated to admit that she ordered her life around Tim, but there it was. She hated when he was there, and the quiet time before he came down was ruined by anticipation.

She heard his feet on the stairs from the loft. She looked at her paper.

"Morning gorgeous," he said. Some mornings he came downstairs furious, some chipper. He touched the side of the coffee pot. "Cold. Christ, Mayla," he said, "how can you drink this stuff?"

"Practice," she said. No one really drank coffee at boiling, not even in Los Etas. Tim had a special coffee maker in the loft. He didn't really need to use the kitchen but most mornings he did. Mostly to bitch about her coffee. He said he didn't like Caribbean coffee, that it was bitter and weak. She didn't like surface coffee, it tasted wrong, bland. And on the surface coffee stayed too hot, too long.

He rummaged around the cupboards while she read about Mandatory Sterilization for Incorrigibles, particularly women who were addicted to neuro-stimulation. He was looking for the jar he used every morning. "Why don't you use that vacuum thing in the loft?" she asked.

He found the jar. She kept pushing it to the back of the cupboard but he kept finding it. He poured coffee in and tightened the lid.

"One of these mornings it's going to explode," she said.

"Nah," he said. The coffee boiled almost instantly, frothing until it filled the jar. He left it, letting it build up pressure, a tiny little storm of coffee.

Mayla could sympathize with the jar. Don't, she thought. Just relax, don't let him get to you. If it breaks, then it breaks. The worst that would happen was that it ruined the flash. She could buy a new flash.

The jar didn't break, it never had yet. Jars didn't break for the Tims of the world, she reflected. If she stuck a jar in the flash there would be coffee everywhere. It would look like the scene of a murder. The flash binged and he pulled it out, opened the lid and the room smelled of coffee. He had to hold the jar with a dish towel to pour. "Ah," he said. "That's what coffee should be. You know, cold coffee is what destroyed the Roman Empire."

She nodded, pretending to look at the paper. Mandatory Sterilization, the headline she had already read. Too late, she thought, he's already born.

"Oh," he said, eyebrows quirked. "Cranky this morning."

"I've run out of things to say about coffee," she said. Her voice was flatter than she intended.

Tim just turned from her and sipped his coffee. The only way he knew how to talk to people was to joke.

She waited for him to say something. If Tim wasn't talking he was mad. "Want the sports?" she asked.

He shrugged.

Another long pause. He wasn't going to be here much longer. She could be polite. "How are the driving lessons going?" she offered.

"Okay," he said, his back to her while he fiddled with his coffee. Now he wouldn't talk in the car, either. She should just enjoy it when he didn't talk but she never could. He had all this energy in the morning—he had all this energy, period—but mornings she was murky and he was ready to fight, to be angry.

"Maybe David could drive this morning?" she said.

He shook his head. "I dunno," he said. "He really isn't ready, yet."

"Ready for what?" she said. "He gets on the belt and puts it on automatic, and when he comes off the belt he's at the bank." She certainly sounded cranky. She wanted to sound reasonable.

"He can't drive very well yet," Tim said.

"This way he could get some practice."

"Give him a break, Mayla," Tim said, sounding aggravated.

"Give *me* a break," she said.

"What is your *problem* this morning?" he said, turning around.

"I want David to drive the car," she said. Take your place, she was saying, and he knew it.

"And you don't give a damn whether he's ready or not," Tim said. "Fine."

"You wouldn't say he was ready if he could—" she couldn't think of an example of expert driving, her mind didn't work in the morning, "—if he could, I don't know, drive like a race car driver."

"Fine," he said again. "And what am I supposed to do?"

"Go back to bed," she said, "enjoy the time off."

"Hijo de la chingada," he said. "Son of a bitch." Except that no one but an anglo would use it that way. When Tim swore in Spanish he sounded even more like a foreign *gabacho* than he normally did.

He would be gone in a month, she told herself. A month, at the most. As soon as David was ready to take over.

When she told David that he would be driving that morning he looked uncomfortable. He came out to the kitchen to get a coffee cup—unlike Tim *he* used the coffee maker in his rooms. He was dressed but his hair was still wet and slicked back from the shower.

"You don't have to unless you feel ready," she said. "Tim can drive me."

"Oh," he said. Which wasn't really an answer. It was hard to be sure how good his English was. He spoke pretty well but sometimes she got the feeling he was nodding without understanding. But he didn't say he wouldn't drive and he was waiting in the kitchen when she was finished getting ready.

He drove cautiously and he seemed to regard stop signs as little time outs. He got to the intersection at the end of her street, stopped the car and sighed, then carefully looked around and drove on. She wanted to turn on the news but felt that if she moved she would distract him, so she decided to wait until they were on automatic. He was all white knuckles getting onto the beltway until he could reach forward and punch 2 on the automatic guidance— preprogrammed for the bank. Then he sighed again.

The news was still talking about mandatory sterilization for incorrigibles and what a wonderful idea it was and how it would work to break the cycle of poverty. That was the only thing she had read in the newspaper this morning so she half-listened and half-watched traffic. At least David's silence was language-related, not directed at her.

"—Danny Tumipamba, an executive in a subsidiary of Marincite Corp.," the news said. The name snagged her.

"Although there is no confirmation from Marine Security, it is widely believed that radical extremists are behind the killing. If so, Tumipamba would be the seventh Marincite executive to fall victim in the last nine months."

"I know him," she said, startled into speaking out loud.

"I am sorry?" David said, not having heard her. Or maybe not having understood.

"Shhh!" she said, but they were talking about someone named Ybarra who'd been killed ten weeks ago. "I know him," she said. "The man in the news. I am working with him on a bank deal." Her Marincite deal, a very big bank deal.

"He was arrested?" David asked.

"No," she said, "He's dead. He was murdered." Murdered. It seemed melodramatic when she said it. Tumipamba was murdered. She knew someone who had been murdered. Had anybody at the bank heard?

"He was a friend of yours?"

"No," she said. Not a friend at all. Danny Tumipamba had a broad Mayan face and hook nose; a face like the Olmec man. He was hard to work with because she never knew where she stood with him, or what he thought of either her or the bank. And now he was dead. A bomb? she wondered, or shooting? She should have been paying attention.

"I'm sorry," David said uncertainly, but the car was slowing down to come off the beltway and his attention was taken by the intricacies of driving.

She didn't have the deal yet, they had still been courting. No papers signed. And now he was dead. Another dead executive in Marincite City, Christos, was it open season on executives over there?

She tried to think of how she felt. Murdered. Dead. Tumipamba was dead.

Dead was something that she didn't understand when someone told her. It was like when her Gram had died, it was the little habits of thought that made her understand

Gram was dead. Like thinking that she had to call Gram, she hadn't talked to her in—and then when she started to think about how long, when she started to really think about it, she'd realized that Gram was gone.

Danny Tumipamba was dead. She didn't have a deal with Marincite yet. She needed that deal.

She would have to talk to her boss. She would have to find out who was taking Tumi's place. She couldn't call this morning, the place would be coming apart. The bank should send flowers, she should find out when the funeral was going to be.

If she was going to get the loan with Marincite Technical Exchange she was going to have to find out who would be deal making.

Maybe she could go to the funeral and see who represented the company. At the funeral she might be able to talk to someone, get a sense of how things might shake down. A couple of hours in a sub, and if the funeral was early she could go in the morning and come back in the afternoon. She would only lose half a day. David could go with her, there was no driving in Marincite. She wouldn't have to take Tim at all.

Tumipamba's funeral was on Thursday morning, two days after he died. Attending meant that Mayla and David had to catch a sub to Marincite City at 6:30 a.m.

Marincite was a labyrinth.

On the map it was a lot of overlapping circles, hubs with roads leading away from them, so the map looked like a drawing of bicycle wheels lying helter-skelter.

It was Mayla's experience that Marincite was an easy place to get lost in. It was older than the capital, and it wasn't a planned city at all. Once it had been a cluster of mining complexes and fish farms, each one dug into the bedrock. Some of them were a single level, some of the mining complexes had been cones going down six or eight levels. Now they were all neighborhoods, overlapping circles, and the streets ran every which way, from hub to neighborhood hub to neighborhood hub.

The funeral was at the Cathedral St. Nicolas in a neighborhood called Wallace. From the sub port they took a shuttle to a place called Sauteuse, and from Sauteuse David used her map to get them to Wallace. He was quite good with the map. Good sense of spatial relationships, she supposed.

The last moving sidewalk dumped them off at a security post manned by Marine Security. *Les Tontons,* "The Uncles." A young man in Marincite maroon stopped her and asked her business. He had that Marincite sound, slightly deeper than Julia. Not surface but different. Everybody's voice was a little deeper in Marincite because it was about twenty meters higher and the air mix was different. He checked her smart card in his reader and flicked a light pen in her eyes for a retinal scan.

David was wearing the gray suit he'd arrived in. Have to have him get some clothes, she thought. He was a skinny little Asian. With his long hair, the suit made him look like a Hong Kong hood in an outdated vid.

He dropped David's smart card in his reader. "I'm sorry, ma'am," he said, "Marine Security records show your security to be a man named Tim Bennet."

"He used to be," she said, "but David has replaced him. I'm sorry, I didn't realize I needed to let you know."

"Without clearance I cannot let him attend you," the young man said. He handed David his smart card with the air of someone finished with a transaction.

"Wait," she said, "Tim doesn't work for me anymore. I have to take David."

The officer frowned, all sharp cheekbones under his polished visor. He looked Haitian. He checked his reader, and then looked icily from under his visor. "His account is still active and linked with yours, so you're still paying him."

She hadn't known they were going to check bank accounts. Now she looked as if she were lying to Marine Security.

"He will be leaving in about four weeks," she said. "But David's account is linked with mine, can't you check that?"

No, he wasn't interested in checking on David, that would take a search which would tie up his reader for a few minutes. The trace to Tim's account was already in place from when Marincite Corp. had registered them.

He was pissed with her, too. Great, just what she needed, problems with *Les Tontons.* Security was everywhere in Marincite; sneeze and an Uncle said, "Good Health." "I really have to go to this funeral. Is there some way I can get clearance?"

"You can go," the officer said. "He can't."

Her insurance said she wasn't to attend public functions in her capacity as a banker without security. But the Cathedral was obviously secure, and who was going to tell the insurance company? Unless she did something stupid like fall down the escalator and broke her leg.

She fumbled with her purse. "Look," she said to David, "go get yourself a cup of coffee, come back in—" how long would a funeral take? An hour? "—an hour and a half."

"Wait," he said. "The problem is what?"

"Marine Security doesn't have any record of you," she said. She didn't want to be late, she wanted to get there early to see if she could maybe talk to Owen Cleary, Tumi's assistant, and she didn't want to explain all this to David. "Take this," she pushed money at him, "find yourself a place to get breakfast or something." She hadn't had breakfast, either. She could never eat when she first got up, but she was hungry now. Oh well, you weren't supposed to have breakfast before mass, anyway. Even if she wasn't Catholic anymore.

"Excuse me," David said to the officer. He pulled out a passport folder and opened it, it was full of his documents.

"I have here my papers, no? I have a work permit, here, see, Ms. Ling's name? She is my employer?"

The officer shrugged.

"Also," David pulled out a flimsy, "here, it is my, what do you call it, like a permission, *autorisation,* to drive a car. See, she has insurance, you know? The insurance says she must have a driver? She, she has paid for my insurance to drive her car, here is her signature? Why would she bring me, arrange this permission to have a car, if I am not her security?"

The officer frowned.

David handed him the folio. The officer didn't want it, he held up his hands as if he were going to say no but David pushed it on him and he took it without really wanting to. Then he didn't seem to know what to do with it. He read the driving permit, paged uncertainly through the passport and ran his pen across the information band. Finally he held it up so he could compare David against the im.

He sighed and handed David back the documents. "All right, but you'll have to wear a telltale. It'll take awhile to get one up here, wait over there, please."

David nodded to the officer and to her, a crisp, know-your-place-in-the-hierarchy kind of nod.

"That was good," she whispered.

"It is like being in the army," he whispered. "If you make it easier for them to do it than not to do it, then they will do it." Then he grinned at her, a sharp little grin.

She grinned back. He was smart, she thought. Smarter than he liked to let on.

She liked that. She could live with that. Once she got rid of Tim, maybe things would work out pretty well.

The telltale was a plastic strip like a hospital bracelet. "Don't fiddle with it," the officer said, "it has a dye packet in it. If you try and take it off, it explodes. The bracelet will let us keep track of you, and it can be triggered either by a security officer or by passing a sensor."

"Where are the sensors?" she asked.

The officer shrugged. "Banks, checkpoints."

David turned his wrist over studying it, then shot his cuff over it to hide it. He didn't look happy. Mayla couldn't blame him.

They took an escalator down. She checked the time. Probably too late to get a chance to talk to someone, maybe after the funeral she could find Owen Cleary for a moment.

The courtyard in front of the cathedral wasn't empty yet so mass hadn't started. The courtyard was bordered by rows of columns etched with palm leaves and capped with cherubim. Behind them were people in dark clothes and headsets. The Uncles, watching and listening.

Too late, Tumipamba was already dead.

David was watching the Uncles, too. "Why so many police?" he asked.

"Tumi was murdered by extremists," she said. She had told him he was murdered—proof that his English really wasn't very good, he missed a lot.

David frowned, "Say again?"

"Murdered by extremists. You know, terrorists. The radical arm of *La Mano de Diós,* the Catholic Socialists." Or some other splinter group, but *La Mano de Diós* was as good an example as any, there were a lot of Catholic Socialists.

"He was a politician?"

"No," Mayla said. "He was an executive for a subsidiary of Marincite Corporation. Marincite Corporation runs this city, it's a company town, so some of the radical groups have started targeting executives."

She wasn't sure how much he had followed but he was intent on her. "This man who is murdered, he is a *zaibatsu* for Marincite?" he asked.

"I guess," she said. She didn't really think of Marincite

as a *zaibatsu* kind of corporation, sing the company anthem and live in a company enclave—Marincite wasn't an enclave for corporate types, it was a city.

"You are in danger?" he asked.

"Me?" she asked.

"Like this man," he gestured towards the cathedral.

She resisted the impulse to laugh. "No," she said. "I'm just a banker, not CFO for a company."

"I am not a person who can protect you," he said. "I think this is a mistake. I was security for the Consulate, but that is just sitting at a desk, watching the monitors. That is just walking around the building, closing the doors."

"It's only insurance," she said. She looked up at the church, suddenly nervous. Funerals. When she was a little girl at school they went to all the funerals during school hours. She never thought anything about them then except that they were longer than regular masses. When they were schoolchildren they attended so many funerals that they knew all the responses. They knew them better than anyone except the priest and the sisters.

"It is not right," he said.

Her Gram had been buried on a Saturday. Schoolgirls in blue uniforms had not said the responses at her funeral. Not that many people had attended: a couple of old men from when De Silva was Minister of Finance and her grandfather had been a *persona de influencia.* De Silva had come. The skin on her grandfather's hands had looked like crumpled paper.

David was looking at her, demanding more. Explain, his face said, explain.

"It's just insurance," she said again vaguely.

The church was like the churches from her childhood, white walls climbing to clerestory windows. Light angled down from the east windows, sharp and brilliant columns that marched up the center of the nave as if this were the surface and the sun were shining in. Such an unnatural hard-edged light that when Mayla was little she thought it was the light of the saints.

They were going to be late if they didn't go in and get seats. At the end of the nave the altar was outlined in tiny blinking colored lights. When she was in school in New York she only saw those lights at Christmas. The white coffin was tilted at an angle and faced from the waist up in glass, so the deceased could watch the mourners come in. She couldn't see Tumi looking at her, from where they stood the light reflected off the glass in a glare of white.

"Look," she said, "we'll talk about it later, okay?"

He stood, all tense, not wanting to let it go and for a moment she thought he wouldn't. Were the Uncles watching them squabble? But he softened and they went in.

They sat on the side, close to where the votive candles flickered in blue and white jars in front of the statue of the virgin. An Erzulie-Virgin, she noticed, a Haitian voudoun madonna in a lace veil and white dress embroidered with rose-colored flowers and hearts. She wore ropes of pearl necklaces and Mayla thought that her wedding ring might actually be Erzulie's three gold rings. The pillars that flanked her niche were striped blue and rose and white, the colors of the loa. Under the candles on the hard concrete floor were a bar of perfumed soap and a handful of wilted pink carnations.

Some woman asking for help in her love life? At home in Julia they would never allow it, never allow any of the signs of Haitian voudoun in the church. She had heard rumors that the execs who ran Marincite Corp asked advice of the loa but it was hard to imagine Tumipamba bringing rum to a mambo in a white headcloth. Even harder to imagine Tumi ecstatic, possessed by spirits.

The priest wore white vestments, like Easter. "Behold, I tell you a mystery," he read, his arms out and his head bowed. "We shall all indeed rise again: but we shall not all be changed." He was a very young man and his hands trembled slightly. The gestures of priests were always effeminate.

After the mass she got in line to pass the coffin. Owen Cleary, Tumi's assistant, stood on the left and a woman with Tumi's square face and Mayan nose stood on the right. Mayla smoothed the folds out of her dress from where she had been sitting.

Owen was white and tired. "Good of you to come," he said when he shook her hand.

"It's a shock," she said and glanced at the coffin but only saw the wash of white. She turned around and a young woman dressed casually in tights and a sweater was taking an im. For the paper? Mayla wasn't supposed to have her picture in the paper, especially not at a funeral for a man murdered by radical extremists.

But the woman had already picked up her bag and was backing down the aisle, and Mayla couldn't think of what she would have said anyway. The woman would have taken other ims. The Uncles were probably taking ims, too.

And then she was out in the atrium with its angel-headed columns and David was coming out to find her. That was it. She had come all the way from Julia by sub to shake Owen's hand. And Owen probably wouldn't even remember she had been here.

She looked around hoping to catch sight of someone to talk to, something to make this trip worthwhile, but she didn't see any familiar faces. People were clustered and the Uncles were standing against the walls like kabuki stagehands. The family would go on back to the house, Owen would probably go, too.

David was waiting for her to tell him what next.

She looked back down the length of the church, at the shafts of hard white light falling at angles. Dust glittered in the light. Imagine light so bright that dust glittered. "Let's go home," she said.

He patted his pockets and came up with their tickets for

the sub and showed them to her. At least, she thought, she hadn't had to deal with Tim. And once David understood that she wasn't likely to be the subject of terrorist attacks he seemed as if he'd do the job very well. He had a sense of propriety about him, he kept his distance. In the evening she would be able to sit in her living room and not worry about Tim.

Privacy! She had built a house and she had no privacy! It was almost as bad as living with her grandfather.

Which made her think of Gram and the dust glittering. The mote in God's eye. She had never understood that before and now she'd seen it, bright dust motes in a column of light. She felt lightheaded—not physically so much as her thoughts skittered around.

"Excuse me," a man said.

David came around, wary. The man was dressed like an exec, a *gabacho,* what the Marincite people called a *blanc,* North American looking with his black suit and his pale face and wavy brown hair. "I don't believe we've met," he said. "Were you a friend of Danny's?"

"A business associate," she said. "I'm Mayla Ling, from First Hawaiian of Caribe."

"Polly Navarro," he said, putting out his hand. "I didn't think I recognized you from the family."

The name sounded half-familiar and she thought she might be supposed to remember who he was. "I'm sure it must be a shock."

"I've been to too many funerals this year," he said. "Makes me wonder if one of these days I'm going to be the guest of honor." A self-deprecating smile, as if it was really in bad taste to say anything so blunt.

And then she connected the name. Not Polly, *Polito.* Polito Navarro. Chief Financial Officer for Marincite Corp. A man who had good reason to wonder if he was going to be the next corpse. Her mind went completely blank. Say something, she thought, anything.

"You were good friends with Danny?" she managed.

He shrugged. "I've known Danny for almost twenty years."

The paper had said Tumipamba was shot leaving for work in the morning. "They're saying it was *La Mano de Diós,*" she said. "Does that mean that they've made some progress towards an arrest?"

"There will be an arrest," he said.

She knew what he meant, that there would be an arrest even if all the evidence was fabricated.

What was Polito Navarro doing wandering around out here by himself? Then again, the place was crawling with security, he could hardly be said to be by himself.

"They're saying the usual," he said, "that it was dissident elements, but Danny might have had some large debts. It may have been his gambling."

Tumipamba was a gambler? Quite a scandal if the CFO of a Marincite subsidiary was killed over gambling debts—not that it would ever come out. Why was Navarro telling her all this? "I'm sure Marine Security will get to the bottom of it," she said. Trite and pious.

"They should have known before it got to this," he said. And told him, he meant. Like a Medici prince, he was part of the ruling family, he should know. There might be a shakedown among the Uncles before this was all over. "Wasn't Danny working on the MaTE division business with you?"

She and Danny Tumipamba had been talking about First Hawaiian providing the funds to allow Marincite Technical Exchange to buy itself from Marincite Corp. Then as an independent company it would turn around and continue to provide services for the parent corporation. It was a complicated deal because in order to amass the capital to buy itself off, Danny had intended MaTE to purchase another company and then strip mine those assets to fund its own independence. MaTE was nowhere near the size of Marincite—Marincite was as big as a small country—but the amount of capital it intended to borrow from First Hawaiian was more by far than any other deal First Hawaiian had ever funded.

It was more money than First Hawaiian was worth. If the buyout didn't succeed, then technically the debt would swallow First Hawaiian whole. It would be bigger than all of First Hawaiian's assets combined, including not only its capital reserves but even the building the bank was in.

But it was not much money at all to Marincite Corp. If Marincite Corp. would guarantee MaTE's assets, then if the buyout didn't succeed, Marincite Corp. would assume the loan.

"I'd like to talk about the MaTE division," Polly Navarro said. "At a more convenient time," he added.

"Oh, yes," she said. She had a card, although it took her a long embarrassing moment to dig it out. "I'd like that very much."

"I'd like to work with First Hawaiian."

"Mr. Navarro," she said, "First Hawaiian would like very much to work with you."

"It would get my good friend Enrique Chavez off my back," he said and laughed. "He's always telling me that Marincite has a duty to return capital to Caribe."

Enrique Chavez was the Government Minister of Finance. "Well, I think you should take the Minister's advice," she said.

He was amused.

"At a better time, then," she said and offered her hand.

"Yes," he said. "I'll be in touch."

He walked back towards the church. One of the big wooden doors was closed and St. Ulrique clutched his fish and looked down at them while St. Patrick thrust his hand out and snakes writhed down the center of the door. Both St. Patrick and St. Ulrique had distinctly Caribbean features.

"We are in the way," David said.

They were standing close to the escalator and people had to cut around them. Riding the escalator up, she

watched for Navarro to come back out of the church.
Maybe he was going back to the house with the family.

What luck. It proved she was right to have come. Not
that anyone had said she shouldn't but before she had run
into Navarro she had felt as if she had wasted the bank's
time and money.

Milagroso. Miraculous.

At the top of the escalator David headed towards the
checkpoint.

"We don't—" she started until she saw him hold out his
wrist. The telltale. She had forgotten. She had been about
to say that they didn't need to check out. Where was her
mind?

She wished she could tell her Gram about meeting with
Polly Navarro. It was an accident, she would have said,
Gram, it was just luck.

You make your own luck, her Gram would have said.

Not really. When her Gram was alive she probably
wouldn't have told her about it. It was bank business and
she never told Gram much about bank business. Church
made her sentimental. You can take the girl out of the
church. . . .

If they hurried they could catch the sub that left ten minutes after the hour and be back in Julia in about three
hours.

David was still standing at the checkpoint, talking to the
woman officer. Hadn't the officer been a man before?
Don't walk over, she thought, let David handle it. But he
looked around for her and then she had to go see what was
wrong.

"The officer who put it on," he said, "he has left."

"He must have taken the deactivator with him," the
woman said. The checkpoint was small, a little booth only
chest high in front. "Titon must have had it on his clip, I'll
call him." She tugged the mic on her headset up and stuck
her finger in her ear. She spoke softly, half-turning away
from them so they couldn't hear.

"The officer is in Castle," she said. "It'll take him awhile to get here."

David was waiting to see what she wanted to do. "Do you suggest we wait?" she asked. Damn it, why was it that when she hired people to take care of things for her she still ended up taking care of them herself?

The officer thought it would probably be about thirty minutes. Which meant they would miss the next sub. "Okay," Mayla said. There weren't any benches around.

"Maybe," David said, "we should get a cup of coffee?" To the officer, "Is there some place? To get coffee?"

The officer thought that there might be a place at the hub. David looked at her to see if she approved. Fine with her, she was delighted to see him take the initiative. "Lead on," she said.

"If I go past, there is no, how do you say," he held out his wrist, "it will not make it go off?"

The officer shook her head, there was no sensor in the booth.

"What trips it off?" Mayla asked again.

Places like banks, jewelry stores, shops that would have a security system.

"As long as we avoid banks we're basically okay?" Mayla said.

"Pretty much," the officer said.

Wallace was a pretty neighborhood. The fronts of the flats were clean and bright: blues or corals to about half-way up and clean whitewashed white above. The windows were covered with ornate grilleworks, metal lattices of roses and leaves or curling vines with butterflies.

They found a café with pseudo-wooden tables and yellow walls with fantastic clocks painted on them. Mayla sat down and found she was worn out. Traveling made her tired. Maybe she wouldn't go back to work, it was going to be late. But she'd call Alex, her boss, and let him know about the meeting with Polly Navarro.

A burro made her feel better. David seemed a little taken aback by the waitress. She wore a peasant skirt and blouse but her hair was bright red and she had ocher and green stripes that ran not just across her eyelids but from temple to temple. War paint. She didn't look very much like a peasant girl in a cantina unless perhaps the cantina was in the infamous neon district in São Paulo.

Still in all, she thought as they walked back to the checkpoint, a little lunch made all the difference in the world.

Riding the pedestrian mover she couldn't see the checkpoint. She checked the time, it was just about thirty minutes, just the time they'd been told to be back. Then she saw that it was lying on its side, folded flat. A crew of three in coveralls was getting ready to load it on a skid. There wasn't any sign of Marine Security.

"They are gone?" David said.

"I don't know," she said and started to walk down the moving sidewalk. The flats fled past them, and then she was stepping off, feeling the strain in her knees as she changed from the speed of the ped mover to solid floor. Two women in maroon coveralls were strapping the folded checkpoint to the skid and a third, wearing a headset, was supervising.

"Excuse me," Mayla said to the stocky woman in the headset. "We were supposed to meet an officer here?"

The woman looked at her. "No officer here now. We are all closed up now."

"No," Mayla said, "they told us to be here now. My security man has a telltale on and someone was going to be here to take it off."

The woman looked at David. "I don't know nothing about that," she said.

"Can you call and check?" Mayla said. She didn't want to get irritated. If she got irritated they'd never get anything done.

"The officer," David told the woman, "his name is Titon."

She looked at David as if she wasn't sure about him, then pulled her headset mic up. "This is Lupe at Sant Nic," she said. "I got two people here say they are waiting on an officer named Titon." She listened, eyes on nothing. Her hair was cornrowed, with little silver fish at the end of each short braid.

"I'm sorry," she said, not sounding particularly concerned. "We are just maintenance, my dispatcher does not know about the uniforms."

David looked at Mayla, sighed. "Maybe there is someplace we should go. Nearby is there a post, for police?"

"You mean a police station? On Tarrou."

"Where is Tarrou?" Mayla asked.

The woman waved vaguely back in the direction they came. "Down three levels at the hub," she said. To the other woman she said, "Is it secure?"

Streets radiated off hub in all directions. "Are you going that way?" Mayla asked.

"No," the woman said and turned her back on them.

David looked at the woman, looked at Mayla and shrugged. He pulled out his map and started pulling off overlays to find Tarrou. "Not this hub," he said after a moment, "I don't think. Excuse me," he said to the woman. "Tarrou, it is not from this hub, is that right?"

The woman did not even look at the map. "I have to work," she said. The checkpoint was secured and one of the women sat down on it. The woman with the headset got in front and the third woman sat down next to her.

David said something in French which did not sound polite.

"I agree," Mayla said.

The woman with the headset started the skid and turned it in a tight circle.

There was no evidence that the checkpoint had ever been there.

"So, we wait," David said, watching the skid putter off. "How long, do you think?"

"Maybe we should call," Mayla said. She didn't see a callbox but they could probably call from the café where they'd gotten the burro. Of course, if they went back there, Titon or whatever his name was could show up and leave. David could go with her and she could call. Or they could use the map and try to find Tarrou.

"There's a police station in the port," she said. "Why don't we just go there and have them take it off?"

He shrugged again.

"If we wait we could be here for hours," she added.

He shook his head. "They are always this efficient?"

"A lot of things are like this," she said.

He checked the map to see how they got back to the port and she let him lead.

Better than Tim, she thought on the ped mover as the flats slipped by. Tim would be blustering.

David looked surreptitiously at the telltale and then pulled his sleeve over it to hide it.

The way back to the municipal shuttle seemed shorter than when they had come in the morning. The waiting area wasn't crowded but the shuttle wasn't in, either. She fumbled through her purse until she found change for the turnstiles. Just beyond they triggered a VR ad and the air was suddenly full of electric blue butterflies. The shimmer was irritating and the focus was off because the butterfly flock was without depth. She ignored them and as soon as she passed out of range they disappeared.

She glanced over her shoulder in time to see David walk into them. He started, raising his hands against the empty air.

"They are allowed?" he said when he had gotten through. "In France, they are not allowed in a public place."

A good idea, she thought. She didn't like them and every so often she read where a tracking laser had burned some-one's eyes. The walls were covered with advertisements. There were butterflies in a lot of them: women in carnival costumes with yellow gauze wings, women's faces painted with wings so their eyes became eyespots, the electric blue butterflies, this time alighting on a flash unit, wings scintillating as they settled and then flickered off, the advertisement tirelessly repeating. Why so many butterflies, were they this year's gimmick?

David sat down next to her, slouched on the bench studying his shoes. He looked very foreign in the suit. Of course he looked pretty foreign anyway. He really needed some new clothes. She should say something but she didn't want to insult him.

The people in the waiting room were the flotsam of midday. There were women who worked the evening shift, old women with their shopping bags, old men in old sweaters and tights that bagged under their knees and around their ankles. A group of boys who should have been in school stood by the door talking and laughing. They wore divers' vests that bared their long ropey arms. A crew. One had a leather demon mask hanging from a seal by a leather thong. The mask was supposed to mean something, it was some kind of rank. At least according to the vid.

David was watching the boys, too. "Why aren't they cold?"

"Pyroxin, probably."

He looked at her sideways, he didn't understand.

"It's a drug. Makes your metabolism burn higher. Divers take it."

He sort of sat up. "You don't get cold?" Interested. Surface people were always cold.

She shook her head, grinning. "It's illegal. Don't even think about it."

He gave an exaggerated sigh and she laughed. She liked him. He could be funny when he wanted to. Once his English got a little better he'd do fine.

The metal door was the size of the door on her garage. As it pulled up, the boys ducked under, but everybody else waited until it was all the way up. The embarcadero was lined with advertisements and she could smell seawater from the surfacing pool.

They walked through the door and there was a sharp crack and David shouted, a hoarse startled shout.

"What—" Something red, bright arterial red, spattered the floor and her side. She shrieked. David crouched, one arm across his eyes and his whole front and left side was covered in red. She thought, *Diós mio,* he's hurt. He's been hurt, there was so much red, so much blood, all over him.

This is bad, she thought.

There was an acrid, eye-watering smell.

Astoundingly he was crouching there, not fallen, but there was so much blood she didn't want him to turn around. There had to be something bad if there was that much hurt and she didn't want to see it, and she stepped back a bit more and her back was against the wall.

She started coughing, David was coughing, still holding one arm over his eyes. Her eyes were watering furiously, tears blinding her.

Pinche tear gas. It was the telltale. He had his right arm held straight out away and behind him. The telltale had gone off. It wasn't a bomb.

People in maroon were running towards them shouting at them in English and Creole. She saw a gun drawn. Mother of God don't let them shoot, she thought, it wasn't her fault. "It's a mistake!" she wheezed. Her throat hurt and she kept coughing. David was shouting in French, still holding his right arm over his eyes, and three Marine Security officers had their guns drawn on him. But he was all right, she thought, as long as they didn't shoot him he was all right.

"It's a mistake," she said and coughed again.

"Shut the fuck up!" an officer yelled, wheeling on her with gun drawn. Just like the vid, she thought, and shut up.

* * *

David's wrist was burned where the telltale had gone off, and his eyes were bloody red from the gas. His suit was completely ruined. The Uncles gave him a pair of maroon overalls to wear and gave him his suit in a sealed plastic bag. He came out to the waiting room with his hair slicked down from the shower and his eyes on the floor.

"Are you okay?" she asked.

He looked up at her with his red eyes, furious, but didn't say anything.

"I'm sorry," she said, thinking, it wasn't really her fault. What could she have done? The Uncles had just lectured her for an hour on how they should have waited for the officer to come to the checkpoint. Her dress was ruined. She'd buy him a new goddamn suit.

"They said we can go now," she said, her voice small.

He nodded. His left hand was still faintly red from the dye.

Maybe she should have said they should wait, but the woman at the checkpoint hadn't said anything about sensors at the shuttle ports, just banks. He could have insisted they wait.

Outside the station they stepped on the ped mover. He didn't say anything the entire trip to the port. He glanced up at her once, with his red furious eyes. They looked ghastly. Her eyes ached, too. But his eyes hurt to look at.

At the sub port he had to open the plastic bag and find the tickets in the wreckage of his suit. Her eyes started watering. The tickets were red and stank. "I'll take them," she said.

He waited while she explained to the ticket clerk what had happened, and the clerk ended up punching her another set and throwing out the ones she had.

She came back and sat down beside David. "Are you all right?" she asked.

He nodded. Then he sighed. "It was a mistake," he said.

She asked him what he meant, but he just shook his head and wouldn't explain any further.

3

Probation

On Saturday David drove Mayla to see her grandfather.

"I am thinking," he said in the car, "I am not the person to do this job for you."

"I think you're doing fine," she said. "I expected it all to take some time to settle in."

He thought of the telltale going off. The burn, the shock. For a moment he had felt the dye and thought it was the moment before one knows one is injured, when there is only the shock and the feeling of something wet. "No," he said. "I think it is not a good idea."

She did not say anything and he stole a glance at her. She was looking out at the road. "I'm sorry about the business in Marincite," she said. "That was my fault."

Yes, he thought, it was. "That is not it," he said anyway, "I think I am just not the right person."

"Is it Tim?" she asked. "He'll be leaving."

He shook his head.

"You haven't even been here thirty days," she said. He put the car on automatic and they accelerated smoothly onto the beltway. "Try it another sixty days," she said. "It'll get better."

"I do not think so," he said.

"I can understand your feelings," she said. "Tim is being a prick. And what happened in Marincite, that would shake up anybody."

He shrugged. It would not get better, but sixty days wouldn't really make a difference. "All right," he said.

"Thank you," she said.

She directed him off the beltway and they dropped down to the second level of the city, then onto residential streets.

The street was a great deal like the street Mayla lived on. Just featureless garage doors, no sense of the residences behind the concrete. She had him stop, and she got out and palmed the sensor next to the garage door. For a moment he thought it wasn't going to open, and then the door lifted.

He expected a garage like Mayla's with space for a couple of cars but this space would have easily held twenty. A public garage, like at the bank. He had not thought much about where her grandfather would live in the city. He guessed he had imagined a place like Mayla's, not this huge residence for many people.

There were only two cars: a long car like Mayla's boss rode to work and a sedan. "Park next to the Benare," she said and pointed to the sedan. Her voice echoed off the concrete. Why were there only two cars in the parking? It wasn't a workday.

At the back of the garage were wrought-iron doors on a lift. The iron was worked into figures, tall birds like cranes and palm trees and flowers. Like an ornate bird cage.

They went below the floor of the garage into a lobby. Concrete walls painted white, black and white tiles on the floor. Dusty Greek busts on pedestals like garden statuary.

The space felt cold and disused, even colder than the usual lobby. This whole country seemed built of concrete.

She folded the lift door back and the iron crashed. He followed her across the black and white tiles into a carpeted hallway. The doors were big heavy wood, and set into each one like a porthole was a Chinese blue and white plate, blue willow plates depicting a girl and her lover fleeing her father the angry mandarin. Some of the doors were open. An office that looked unused—so this was not just residential flats. Then a storeroom full of old furniture. Then a bedroom. Just one room, with a bed. Like a hotel room almost except there was bric-a-brac all over the table: glass harlequins on a lace doily, feather masks on the wall and a handful of medicine bottles on a glass dish. An old woman's room.

Bedsitters? Rich daughter letting old grandfather live in poverty—although the place didn't feel impoverished, just empty and ugly and full of old people's used things.

He followed her down five steps and across a large room with dining tables and chairs draped in white cloths. The walls were mirrored, reflecting back white-shrouded furniture. Community dining?

"Jude?" she called.

The place made him uncomfortable, with its empty concrete rooms. Maybe it was being closed down or something? She had not said anything about having to move her grandfather, but then she hadn't said anything at all about him.

"Jude?" she said again, and he followed her through a door into a kitchen. Just a kitchen, good sized, with a wooden table and chairs and a shiny yellow tile floor. The black man mopping the floor said, "Don't you step on my floor, miss."

"Jude," Mayla said.

The man leaned the mop up against the counter and tiptoed across the clean floor and gave Mayla a hug. "Where you been?" he asked.

"I've been busy," Mayla said.

"He's an old man." "Old mon," Jude actually said, in helium falsetto.

"I know, I know. How's his cold?"

Jude shrugged. "The man, he's eighty-two."

"Is he in bed?"

"No, he's out on the spring court."

"Is Domingo with him?" she asked.

The man shook his head. "There's nothing wrong with Domingo. You just feeling guilty, knowing Domingo is taking care of him and you don't get out here often enough."

"I didn't say anything," she said, throwing her hands in the air. They both laughed, as if this was an old thing between them.

"You both staying for dinner?"

"Oh, Jude, this is David Dai, he's working for me. David, this is Jude."

"Where's that other one?" The man's voice was carefully neutral.

"Tim is going back to Australia. We can't stay for dinner this time. Next time, I promise."

David suddenly understood, this was all one house. This was all Mayla's grandfather's house. The lobby, the parking, all the rooms. The dining room draped in white. All empty.

"I'm baking potatoes," Jude said, "not in the flash, neither."

"With real sour cream?" Mayla asked.

"What do you think?"

"Next time," she said. "I promise."

All one house. Huge and ugly and cold.

He followed her again, back out across the empty dining room and up another five steps to a room with mirrors like windows and tables covered with lace and picture frames. Another wooden door with a blue and white plate set in it. Mayla pushed the door open and yellow light spilled out.

The room was full of light and he blinked. The bright air was damp and misty, no, it was misting. Raining. Like rain. Space went up and up; twice, three times the height of the kitchen. There were clusters of plants and in the center of each clump stalks of tall bamboo, four or five meters high. The floor was terra-cotta tile, glazed Indian red with artificial rain. All around the walls, tall mirrors like windows. And in the center was an old man in a wicker chair and a young man holding an old navy blue umbrella.

"Hello," Mayla said, her voice too loud and too cheerful, "over your cold?"

"Nearly," the old man said. He was a flat-faced, long-boned ugly old Chinese man with dyed black hair. At least David assumed it was dyed. "How is the bank?" the old man asked.

"The bank is doing well," she said. "Can you turn off the sprinklers? We're getting wet."

She took the umbrella from the young man—Domingo?—and held it while he went to turn off the sprinklers. "I just got back from Marincite," she said. "Did you read in the paper about Tumipamba's funeral?"

"Jude said your picture was in the paper," her grandfather said.

There had been an im in the paper, of the coffin with Mayla standing at the foot, facing out of the picture. Mayla's presence in the picture was an accident. Crisp black-and-white im, the cliché of funerals. Tim had said she looked like "a frigging presidential widow."

"I went to the funeral." She sounded defensive.

"That was stupid," he said.

"I was working with Tumipamba," she said. "I thought I should go to the funeral."

"And get your picture in the paper?"

"I didn't even know they took the im," she said.

"You were working with this man? In Marincite?"

"We're negotiating an agreement," she said. "With Marincite."

She offered that as a kind of gift, her voice hopeful. The old man was silent, considering.

The rain stopped. David found he'd been hunching his shoulders.

"What kind of agreement?" her grandfather asked. Like his own father, David thought, this was a man who did not trust gifts. Who had to turn them over and over and who always suspected either a bribe or a catch.

"Marincite Technical Exchange is going independent," she said. "Marincite is spinning them off. We may do the financing. A lot of money."

He didn't help her, just waited for her to go on. After a bit of silence she said tentatively, "I offered short-term notes with an automatic rollover. It would have been a better deal for them, but they wanted five-year fixed, something about the way they do business." The terms meant nothing to David but he listened to the sound of her voice. He could hear things better now, through the strangeness of language and the shrillness. He could hear her nervousness, and hear how she got a little less nervous as she talked. She chattered on about buying some buildings and leasing them back to the company, while the old man sat silent, his eyes on the Indian red tile.

"Short term?" he said suddenly, and coughed, a bark. "Why'd you push short term if they wanted fixed?" He had a hard, flat, American voice, David could hear that, too.

"The U.S. market is falling," she said, her voice gone sharp and defensive again, "it's got to correct, and then interest rates will drop. We thought with Marincite we'd have to give them short term. The bank will take short term," she said and shoved her hands in her pockets.

The old man looked up at her. "You didn't do your homework." The old tyrant looked pointedly at her hands and she took them out. "A client shouldn't have to be sold," he said.

She didn't say anything, just took her dressing down. Maybe she knew that nothing would make any difference.

Better than himself, every time he saw his father they ended up screaming at each other. When was the last time he had seen his father?

Mayla's grandfather looked at him. "You're new," he said.

Mayla promptly introduced her grandfather, "John Ling," she said. John Ling leaned forward in his wicker chair and held out his hand and for a moment David thought he was supposed to help the old man stand up. Then he realized the old man wanted to shake hands.

Loose dry skin over fragile bones.

"What happened to the big blond . . . Tim?" the old man asked.

"He's going back to Australia," Mayla said.

"Are you American?" John Ling asked.

Nobody had ever thought he was American before. "No sir," David said. "French."

"Southeast Asia?"

"Yes sir," David said, "Indochina."

"Speak any Chinese?" the old man asked.

"No sir, my grandmother speaks Vietnamese."

The old man sat back. Nodded. "I went to Chinese school after regular school for a couple of years, but I never learned a bit." His attention went back to Mayla. "What are you wearing?"

She had on a red silk blouse belted over tights, something simple and bright, David thought. Although what did he know about how people dressed?

"You spend a lot of money on clothes," he said. "Your grandmother never spent so much on clothes."

She sighed.

The old man stared out at the plants. Was his vision bad? The silence hung.

"So how are you feeling?" she said, trying to fill the space.

"Old," he said. "And helpless."

She looked up at Domingo and then at David, looking for help or for something to say. Her face was pink.

David found he could not meet her gaze, so instead he looked at the bamboo.

"I was thinking," she said in the parking, "maybe we should go someplace for dinner." Her voice was bright, working hard at it. She dug in her purse. "I think, I looked up restaurants . . . but I think the best place . . . wait," she found a piece of paper. "I thought maybe a French restaurant, you know, I thought you might like some food from home."

Food from home. Chicken. Pasta. Something other than fish. "It does not matter," he said. Homesickness washed over him in waves, all he could think of was bread and butter—not tortillas and not that bland stuff from the U.S., just a decent piece of bread. He wanted to go home. Sixty days, he had promised. At the moment it seemed an immeasurable wait.

"I went away to school," she said, "I remember what it was like. Besides, after that business in Marincite, I wanted, you know, I mean I can't make you forget that but—"

"It doesn't matter," he said again.

"It does," she said. "I don't know what to say about it. It was horrible. It was horrible for me, and I wasn't wearing the telltale."

Blind. He had thought he was blinded. The memory was bad, he slid away from it and shrugged.

She looked down at her hands.

He meant only to pass it off, but she looked as if he had shrugged her off. She looked the way she had when she was standing in front of her grandfather.

"I would like to go to a restaurant," he said.

She smiled at him, grateful. How easy to make her happy. "Well," she said, serious again, consulting her scrap of paper, "there are a couple of places but everybody says that the best place is Botticelli's. It's in Aphrodite, that's a casino." She looked down at her piece of paper. "Actually, it's not French, it's Continental. But they have some French dishes and some other things, too. Italian, and Spanish."

"Okay," he said, and was rewarded again by her smile, so he smiled, too. "Okay," he said, to make her smile, to feel his own face mirroring hers.

"Okay," she said.

He nodded, and because he didn't know what else to say, he said it again. "Okay." And it sounded so inane, this dialogue of "okays" that they started to laugh, grinning at each other like idiots. A couple of emotional cripples, he thought. Grinning at her in her grandfather's parking.

Botticelli's was in the middle of the casino. It was dark and each table sat in a little pool of light. For a centerpiece each table had a stand and a live parrot: blue parrots, green parrots, gray parrots, all with heavy bills and strong ugly feet. He looked and was relieved that at the tables where people had food there were no parrots.

The prices made him still. The chicken, the beef dishes were 45cr and 55cr. He looked up and the blue parrot flipped down to hang upside down. A little sign said that they nipped.

"Poor things," Mayla said, "they don't do well in the air mixture, the cold gets them. Most of them don't live long."

He supposed they didn't fly because their wings were clipped, but what kept them from climbing down the stand and onto the table? The parrot turned and twisted its head, snake fashion, then clambered sideways and righted itself, flapping its wings. It opened its beak when a waiter walked by and its tongue was black. It stared at David, flipped upside down again.

A waiter stopped at their table and the parrot righted itself again. The waiter asked if they were ready to order. He had no idea what he wanted, he hadn't even decided if maybe he should order fish—it was the cheapest thing on the menu.

The waiter said he'd be back and fed the parrot a peanut. The parrot craned its head and fluffed out its feathers. It raised its wings and made a "ding" exactly like the sound of a flash unit signaling "ready."

Mayla looked up from her menu.

"It was the bird," David said.

She laughed and the bird stared at her. "They're distracting, aren't they? I think we should get a bottle of wine, but you have to order, I don't have the nerve to order wine in front of a Frenchman. The chicken dishes are famous."

There wasn't much on the menu he had ever eaten before but he didn't tell her that. He ordered *coq au vin* and she ordered some kind of chicken with garbanzo beans so he got a Chardonnay. White with chicken and he liked Chardonnay. Growing up his family hadn't drank wine often, and when he did buy it he usually just got a *vin de table*. He really didn't know much about wine.

The waiter came and got the parrot, whisking the thing away, stand and all. David was relieved.

The food was good, and even if it tasted a little different, it was not fish. It tasted so good he wolfed it down so it never really had a chance to get cold. The bread wasn't bad, warm crusty rolls wrapped in a big napkin, and he sopped his plate clean. He thought the wine was all right and Mayla seemed to think so.

Coffee after dinner, not-hot-enough Caribbean coffee. Then they walked back through the casino.

"Blue and whites," Mayla said suddenly.

He looked at her, not understanding.

"There's been a bomb threat," Mayla said.

David looked around. He saw people at the slot machines, heard the muted whir and chime of gambling, nothing out of place, everything seemed normal. Then he saw, at the door, six in police blue and white.

She sighed. "We could end up standing here for an hour if they've just started a sweep."

The boy who stopped them looked maybe nineteen, with the smooth skin of a young man. Under his lifted visor he had the look David associated with the military: youth and exercise and steady food. Like the young people at the security check in Marincite, except that this boy wore crisp blue and white fatigues rather than maroon and cream. "Excuse me," the boy said, "can I see some identification?"

They passed over their smart cards and the boy dropped them in his reader, then used the image to check, im against face, all six points. Like the port, David thought, so thorough. He consciously loosened his shoulders.

"Is it a bomb threat?" Mayla asked.

"No ma'am," he said. "An arrest. But we don't know if the suspect is here to place a bomb or not, so we are being very careful. Could you stand over there for a moment?"

Mayla seemed to find it normal. This country was crazy, David thought. They stood over at the side of the entrance. How could these people live this way? he wondered. He watched as two men and a woman saw the team and hesitated. It was obviously irritating to have to stand around and wait. He wished they could wait outside, particularly if they thought that someone might be placing a bomb. Then it occurred to him that in a structural sense there really was no outside in Julia. The doors didn't make so much difference. The three people stopped and the woman said something to one of the men. "What can *I* do about it!" the man said. The third man hung back a bit.

They came down and presented their IDs. The woman was tiny and dark, with a triangular face. African, he thought. Maybe she was Haitian, some Haitians were as dark as Africans. Just because he had been in Africa he thought she looked African. She was angry about something, refusing to talk to the man she was with except in clipped monosyllables. "How long will this be?" she asked the boy in blue and white and he shrugged. He thought she sounded African, but he still had problems with the way the air mixture distorted everything.

"You'll have to wait over there," the boy said, pointing at where Mayla and he were standing.

"I wasn't even supposed to be here tonight," the woman said.

Northern Africa, he thought. She didn't look like the blacks he'd fought with in Anzania.

"Over there," the boy said.

She still wanted to argue but the boy shrugged his rifle around and clicked the safety.

He looked at the rifle and then at the woman. The rifle didn't seem to matter to her, but she grimaced and let the man she was with pull her towards the side.

It did not feel dangerous, exactly, surely the boy was just trying to put her in her place, and yet it did. Africa, and rifles in the hands of very young men. After the way things had gone with the telltale, Caribbean Security forces made him nervous.

"Identification," one of the blue and whites said to the man, who had not really been with the couple. At least, now he did not seem to be with the couple, but before, when David first saw them, he thought that they had been. Not because they were talking, or even walking exactly together, but not walking separately. But now it seemed that they did not know each other.

This country, it made him see plots everywhere. Like Tim's diving lesson.

The man handed the blue and white his smart card and the boy dropped it in the reader. David put his hand on Mayla's arm and pulled her further back. He didn't know why, perhaps it was the sound of the safety on the rifle when the boy had been talking to the woman, perhaps it was thinking about Africa, he didn't know.

The boy grabbed the man's arm and wrenched him

around, letting the reader swing on his belt, "DON'T MOVE! NOBODY MOVE!"

The young man said. *"There's been a mistake—"* Always, the same thing they say, he thought, mistake.

"AGAINST THE WALL, MOTHERFUCKER!" the boy shouted, and the other officers were shoving him, too, and the man panicked, swung out. One of them slammed his head against the wall, it made that hollow melon sound, and then they hit him in the kidneys with their rifle stocks.

The young man's nose was bleeding and he was dazed. Blue and whites came running. Blue and whites everywhere. David was backing up, pulling Mayla with him. The young man disappeared in a crowd of blue and whites. At the edge of the blue and whites stood the African woman and her man. They were not backing up, they were watching, their faces blank. The woman had the man's arm, her fingers straining the fabric of his sleeve.

She looked away, looked back at them. She looked at Mayla, who was watching the blue and whites. She looked at Mayla a long moment. David wondered what she was thinking, maybe she did not even realize she was looking at Mayla.

He looked at her, and she glanced at him and looked away.

It was almost an hour later when they finally got their smart cards back. A different officer dropped them each in readers, "Ms. Ling," he said, and handed her hers.

"Mr. Dai."

To the African woman he said, "Ms. Clark?" Odd name, David thought, maybe they are married? But the man's name was James.

They walked back to the parking, to the shining little black car. He was edgy. Paranoia, he thought. The sound of the safety, the age of the boy, the African woman.

"Clark," he said. "Is it a common name, in Haiti?"

Mayla was not paying attention and he had to repeat the question. "Not that I know of," she said.

So the woman was not Haitian, he thought. Maybe she was from a different island. Maybe she was not African, he had trouble with voices here.

The car park was not very big and it was only half full, most of the vehicles were motor scooters, parked all in a row. The Skate was parked beside a delivery skid, invisible from where they came in. But it was there, snug and polished. David found the keys and heard a cry. Small and animal, nearly soundless.

A child, an infant, he thought, and looked up at Mayla. She was looking at him, waiting. "Did you hear it?" he asked.

Before she answered he heard it again. Not a baby, a kitten, from close by. The sound was so helpless it hurt his chest.

He crouched.

The kitten was tiny, hunched next to the wheel. David clucked with his tongue and it mewed again.

"What is it?" Mayla asked.

"A kitten," he said. He wished that it would come out, if the driver of the skid didn't hear it, it would be crushed. "Where are your people?" he asked.

"What?" Mayla said. She crouched down. "I don't see it."

"There," David pointed.

"Ah," Mayla said. *"Pobrecito."*

Yes, poor thing, stuck down here. Caribe seemed an unnatural place for a kitten, never able to sit in the window in the sun.

It took a few tentative steps, its tail a bottle brush. Out in the light it was gray with dirty white paws and belly. It was skinny and filthy. Little refugee. Its eyes had little tiny sores, flea bites? Suddenly it sat, scratched its ear vigorously and shook its head. Ear mites, he thought.

"Where does he come from?" Mayla asked.

"Nowhere," David said. She stood. The kitten scuttled sideways and went back under the skid.

"Is there someplace we can take him?" David said. "You know, people who take care of animals with no people? A *société* for animals?"

Mayla didn't know of such a place.

David clucked again and the kitten mewed. It came a few steps and mewed again, tiny teeth and an astonishing pink mouth. He clucked and wiggled his fingers.

Stiffly the kitten approached him. He coaxed closer, moving his fingers just out of reach, and the kitten stretched to sniff, stopped nervously, came another step—David snatched it up. It grabbed his jacket.

"You'll probably catch something," Mayla said.

"I already have," he said and grinned. He felt absurdly pleased with himself. The kitten clung and mewed.

"What are you going to do with it," she said.

He shrugged. "Maybe I will find someone to take it. A *société* for animals."

She shook her head, "You keep him in your apartment," she said.

"Just for a few days," he said.

"Right," she said.

But she held the dirty little thing on her lap while he drove home.

"What will you call it?" she asked.

"I should not give it a name," he said, "I want to give it to a place where they will take care of it." They would probably kill it, he thought, but that would be better than leaving it to die of neglect. He could not keep it, he was leaving.

"You have to call it something," Mayla said. She was teasing, she was saying that she didn't think he would give it away.

"Call it Mephistofele," he said. "From the opera," he added.

"Well," she said, "he probably will turn out to be a little devil."

He was pleased that she knew the name. "Ah, non," he said, "I was thinking, he will never see the sun."

She looked at him oddly. Foolish thing to say, she lived here, she didn't see the sun much either.

At Mayla's request, Tim took him to get some clothes. They went into a part of town where he had never been. Here the traffic was all motor scooters and bicycles, and they had to park the car and take escalators and walk.

The air was damper here and didn't smell right. David found he kept taking deep breaths. The shops were all small. The shop where Tim took him to buy clothes was a deep narrow place that had once been a restaurant. The flash unit and grill were gone, but the counter and stools were still there and the counter was piled high with stacks of sweaters. The Indian who ran the shop bobbed along behind them.

"Tights," Tim said, "for him."

"Sirs," the Indian said, "what size?"

David didn't know, sizes were different here. He gave his inseam in centimeters and the shopkeeper turned to the wall of shelves and rifled through neatly folded stacks of tights. "Sirs, will you be wanting the new colors? I have bright colors, all very popular."

He gestured towards the wall opposite the counter where shelves were stacked high with neatly folded pairs of tights. Two columns of tights were vivid rainbows: rose madder and cobalt blue and bright hard yellow.

Tim grinned. "No, I don't think so. Just black and gray."

Three pairs of black, three pairs of gray. And sweaters.

David went into the dressing room and tried on tights. They looked cold, the outside was some slick, rubbery-looking material. But the inside was soft, like chamois, and warm. He found a pair of gray that fit. They were wonderful, so much better than pants.

He eyed his reflection. The dressing room was barely big enough to turn around in, but he could still see the effect. Embarrassing. He had not really paid much attention to the way other people looked in divers' tights. Except for at the bank, where the men wore suits, most everybody on the street seemed to wear them.

He had legs like a chicken. Tim did not have legs like a chicken, Tim had broad, strong legs like tree trunks. He did not relish the idea of wearing these around Tim. He considered critically, did they show his bad knee?

Probably, he thought, and sighed. Still, they were warm. Vanity or comfort? Everybody wore them.

He bought a gray pair and a black pair. And four sweaters: a dark green, a navy blue, a kind of olive green and a red one. The last because the red looked so warm. He also bought a pair of sandals. Nobody wore shoes, shoes looked foolish with tights. He stood there in his new tights and the olive sweater, feeling foolish, and tried to sort through the maze of Caribbean currency.

So Tim was amused, he told himself.

Still, on the street with his purchases he felt a little less conspicuously foreign. Tim walked fast, took long strides, and he had to work to keep up. The sandals had no backs and there was a knack to keeping them on; if he wasn't careful he would walk right out of them.

Silly to buy clothes when he wasn't going to stay here. Which made him think of the kitten. It was a bother. He had looked in the directory for a place for animals but there was nothing. But he couldn't take it back to France. It would cost so much. He supposed he would have to have it put down.

Poor little refugee.

Tim would be pleased to know he didn't plan to stay although mostly Tim ignored him. Even walking down the street, Tim paid no attention to him. Like the way he used to ignore his little sister when he was a kid. Or when he was in Blacksburg, and he and Thieu used to run around and ignore his younger cousin. Maybe he could fly to Blacksburg when he left Caribe, see his aunt and uncle and run around a bit with Thieu. Thieu was married and had two, or maybe three children. He would like to see his cousin's children.

It might be awkward. He would write his aunt and ask for Thieu's address.

"To call the United States," he asked Tim, "is it so expensive?"

"I don't know, I've never called the U.S. Why would you call the U.S.?"

"I have family there," David said. "I thought I would like to go see them."

"It probably isn't that expensive. Have you talked to Mayla about time off?"

"No," David said. He didn't think he should say to Tim that he was leaving, he didn't think Mayla wanted Tim to know. Then again, Tim might be a little easier to live with if he thought David was leaving.

Silence might be best.

He did not like secrets. "I do not know if I will take the job," he said. "You know, this is a probationary period. Maybe at the end I will leave."

Tim frowned. "What's wrong with the job?"

"I am not suited, I think," David said.

"It's a good job," Tim said. Which was beside the point.

They got on the escalator. The escalators were awful, dirty and graffitied and this one smelled of smoke on top of a strong odor of urine. At the top of the escalator was a shed that sold sausages. Coals glowed in the bottom of the grill. David thought that fires were illegal in Caribe because they ate up oxygen and put a further burden on the air purification systems.

A whole family seemed to live in the shed: father, mother, a girl about six or seven, and a naked, potbellied little boy no more than three. The little boy had a dirty cord tied around his ankle to keep him from wandering. Flat mestizo faces watched people get off the escalator. Nobody seemed to buy. The little boy alone seemed unconcerned, he stood on a pink blanket gone gray with grime and cooed and crowed to himself.

This country could not take care of its people, there wouldn't be a *société* for animals. Maybe not even veterinarians. What to do with Meph? He could not just abandon him, it would be cruel, but if there was no vet. . . . Could he kill the kitten himself?

There would have to be a vet. Some people, like Mayla, they would have a pet, wouldn't they?

"Is it Mayla?" Tim asked.

"What," David said.

"Why don't you like the job?"

"I don't like this country," David said. A half-truth.

Tim seemed to relax. "Yeah," he said. "I can see that. The place is a mess, isn't it. But Mayla is all right. Sometimes she doesn't know what she wants, you know."

David didn't know, but he nodded.

"Sometimes, she gets me so mad I don't know what to do with her. She changes her mind. One minute she likes you, the next minute she doesn't. I think it's because part of her is North American, like her family, and part of her is Caribbean, and the two sides are at bloody war half the time."

"Why do you stay?" David asked. The question he had been wanting to ask.

"I don't know," Tim said. "I went to Belize and was there for awhile, and then she asked me to come back and she offered me this goddamn job. And then she decided she was mad at me and she wanted to get rid of me. I figure she'll change her mind again."

David did not think so but he didn't see any need to voice an opinion.

"Besides," Tim said suddenly, "Sometime in your life you gotta stick to something, you know?"

A strange statement that left as many questions as it answered. How had he known Mayla before he went to Belize? Why had she asked him to come back?

If David stayed, would she change her mind about him, too?

One more reason why he did not want this job.

It was the easiest job he had ever had. He took Mayla to work, picked her up in the evening. Sometimes he did the grocery shopping. Most of the time he spent in his room, with the kitten, Meph.

In the afternoon, when she wasn't working late, he got to the bank half an hour early and sat in the Skate in the parking, reading. He should have been reading English, to improve. But he didn't like reading English, he read it slowly. The university bookstore had some French novels: Camus, Sartre, Gide, Heureaux. He found a copy of *L'Etranger* (which struck him as an ironic book to sell in a foreign country). He couldn't say he really liked the book, but he had spent over a month in a hospital in Algeria after he had been wounded in Anzania and he liked the descriptions of North Africa, even though he had been in In Salah, in the middle of the desert, rather than Algiers, on the coast.

Someone tapped on the glass. Two people were standing there, a man and a woman. He opened the door wondering if he was late? But it was not yet five, not quite time to go upstairs to get Mayla. Something was wrong with Mayla?

The woman said, "Are you Jean Dai?"

"Yes," he said. She said "Jean" the way they said it in France, not the way they said it in the States. Nobody ever called him "Jean," except people who didn't know him and got his name off of records, like in the military or on the first day of school.

"Could we talk to you?" she asked.

"Is something wrong?" he asked.

"No," she said, "but we would like to discuss some business with you." She was familiar, but he couldn't place her, from the bank, maybe?

"Ms. Ling gets off at five—"

"It won't take long," the man said. He sounded as if his first language was Spanish.

"Would you come with us?" the woman asked. She was tiny, with a narrow face in which all the muscles and ligaments stood clearly on the bones, just underneath skin so dark it almost looked blue under the lights in the parking. "There is a place up the street, a restaurant." She leaned forward and the shiny black plastic crucifix she was wearing dangled between them, the Christ twisted in exaggerated agony.

"Are you with the bank?" David asked. No, not the bank, where had he seen her?

"I think it would be more comfortable to talk elsewhere," she said.

"Perhaps we could talk here," David said. "I would be late." He thought of the handgun in a sling underneath the seat. He had thought it was foolish when Tim showed him.

The man looked at the woman, she lifted her shoulders fractionally. The man sighed and pulled a paper out of his jacket, opened it on the hood of the Skate and leaned on the car. "Is this your employer?"

The paper was a copy of the im that had appeared in the newspaper after the funeral: Mayla in her black dress, looking off the page.

The hood of the car was flexed under the man's weight. "Please do not lean on the car," David said. The man straightened sharply.

"You do not mind if we speak French?" the woman asked. Her accent was clearer in that language, even in falsetto. "It is much more private that way."

He didn't mind. (But he did, she was trying to use him.

"We are the same," she was saying. When he did not even know who she was.)

"Your employer's family came to Caribe before the 'liberation'." She said *"liberation"* fastidiously, her teeth delicate white. "The liberation was supposed to free this country, but the unemployment rate is now higher than it was when Bustamante took power. The housing shortage is more severe than ever, and the construction of the new sixth level is progressing so slowly that by the time it is finished we will need even more housing than we do today. And do you know why? Because of the corruption of high officials who pretend to buy first rate materials and pay labor, when in fact they buy third rate materials and create phantom companies with no real employees and line their own pockets with money. But you work for Ms. Ling, who is a tool of these people, so surely you know this? I am boring you, I am afraid?"

No, she was not boring him.

"You are the woman from the casino," he said, "Clark." She was the woman who had been there when the man was arrested.

The tiny woman clasped her hands together. "The man who was arrested, he is innocent of any crime except the desire for justice for all peoples. Are you aware that almost half of the households in Julia with children under six are single parent households? That forty percent of all the children in Caribe go to bed hungry? That the average family's major source of nutrition is yeast substitutes? And the government lines its own pockets, and banks such as this one loan them the money to do so. They mortgage their own people."

Namibia. Woman and children lined up clutching enamel bowls, waiting for boiled corn. That was mortgaging one's own people and going bankrupt. He didn't like politics; the woman was telling the truth, he thought, but he couldn't be drawn into that just now. He had to think. He was fascinated by the black plastic crucifix swinging between them. It was as long as the palm of his hand, the features of the Christ's face a clearly defined rictus of pain. He had seen crucifixes like that before.

"Here, the rich get clean, dry air. Go down a few levels, Mr. Dai. The air is damp and impure. There is not enough oxygen because the recirculating equipment is old, insufficient for the population and not maintained." She covered the crucifix reverently with her hand, tiny wiry hand with beautiful nails, pink and paler than her skin. "Please come and talk to us, Mr. Dai," she said in English, "we need your help. Our brothers are held in prison with no chance of due process or escape, if we are to free them we must bargain with the government. You can help us turn their own tools against them."

"*Êtes-vous Catholique d'Afrique del Sud?*" he asked. South African Catholics. She was, he recognized the Christ, but what would a member of the South African Catholic and Apostolic Faith be doing in Caribe?

"Divisions within the world church are artificial in the eyes of God," she said. "For centuries the Church has allowed itself to be schismed by internal politics while neglecting the very people it should serve. And now the official church has no more to do with God than this bank." She gestured towards the entrance to First Hawaiian. "But God is in the world, Mr. Dai. God is with us. We are his instrument, and we will set in motion powerful forces. You know, Mr. Dai, that the world is a complex web, and that not one of us draws a breath but that it affects the rest of the world. But God sees the pattern in chaos, and he shows us where to strike. We are God's surgeons, Mr. Dai."

This woman was violence. Here he was, in a city under the ocean (when he pictured Caribe he always thought of an atlas, blue oceans, the Atlantic and Caribbean with the arrows of currents sweeping great circles); here he was, and *Afrique* had followed him on one of those arrows. *Afrique* was making demands on him.

She was still talking. "You are inside, Mr. Dai. You can bring us inside. If we are to free our people, we must place our scalpel in precisely the right place. You can be our hand."

He nodded. Go away, he thought, leave me alone.

Her eyes were huge, hungry. The face of the South African Irregular Forces, who sometimes fought with the Republic, sometimes with the Prots. And now that the war was over and the Republic had won, the faces of the people who had lost most of all. "You could help, you could strike a direct blow. I wish I were in your place." She did wish it, her face said desperate things, "help us." It said, "help *me.*" It said, "I am hungry."

He looked at her and she looked at him, holding her black plastic crucifix folded in her small hand with its clean pink nails. This woman wants to die, he thought.

"We are friends," the man said, taking the woman's arm and pulling her back a step, holding her next to him as if to dampen the intensity of her wanting. The weight of their wanting.

David glanced around, checking the exits. Through the Skate's window he saw the book, *L'Étranger,* open and upside-down on the seat. "Excuse me," he smiled, "my book, that isn't good for them." He opened the door and the man tensed, but before they could really do anything, David rested his knee on the seat, closed the book and dropped it between the driver's and passenger's seats. In the mirror he saw the man waiting. David reached under the seat, expecting them to lunge, and for a moment his hand did not find anything but still they did not move. He found the handle of the handgun, smooth and cool, and straightened up. "Please go now," he said, holding it on them.

They stared at him. What was he going to do now, shoot them? Once he had shot a South African Prot less than ten feet away, close enough to see the other's face dissolve. But that was with shooting going on all around, running, the incredible noise of battle. That was a different kind of fear, larger, but less complicated than this fear. He did not know what they would do. He could see the terrible betrayal, the terrible sadness in the woman's face. The man's face was blank and that was worse because he did not know what feeling was behind it, what the man might do.

Should he shoot the man?

Then the man backed up a few steps, pulling the woman with him. She looked as if she might say something.

"I have been in *Afrique*," David said. "I have already paid. Please, just walk."

And then they turned and walked away. Just like that.

He waited, rigid, until they had left the parking, gone across the street, walked out of his line of sight. The im from the funeral—Mayla in her black dress—was still sitting on the hood of the Skate. He picked it up, locked the car and went into the bank.

In the elevator up from the parking he had to figure out what to do with the handgun. He tucked it in the waist of his tights and felt foolish pulling on his sweater as the door opened. "Hello Max," he said to the receptionist. "I have to talk to Ms. Ling."

Max called. She was on a call, just a moment.

"Tell her it is an emergency," David said. Max looked at him and nervously adjusted the cuffs of his suit before calling. David was afraid that in a moment the shaking would creep from his knees to his hands. Max pointed down the hall.

It was the first time he had been in her office. Books, real books, a whole wall of them, and leather chairs. There were overhead lights, but on her desk next to her console was a gooseneck lamp with a green glass shade. "I'll get back to you," she was promising and then she cut off the call.

"Two people in the parking, they just tried to, what do you say, make me join their organization. Politics. They wanted me to do something."

"What two people," she said, "what do you mean?"

"What two people! I don't know these people! They have this, ask me if I work for you!" He thrust the paper at her and she took it, frowning.

"They gave you this?" she asked.

"They left it," he said, "I held the gun on them, told them to leave!" He pulled the gun out of his waistband.

She did not look at it, she looked at him. Like the woman with the crucifix, the weight of her look, wanting something from him. Then she keyed the console. "Police please, Corinne Street District."

He was cold. It was so cold here. It was what came after the adrenaline. He crossed his arms thinking, this is it. This is not the army, I do not have to stay. If I want to I can leave.

"Are you okay?" she asked.

"Cold," he said, furious with her. When she had hired him she did not say anything about this.

She called Max, asked him to bring two cups of tea. "What happened," she said, "what did you do?"

"I told them to go away," he said. He put the gun down carefully on her shiny black desk. She blinked.

"Who are these people," she asked. Looking at the gun.

"A South African Catholic," he said. "The people from the casino, from the arrest."

"From the arrest?" she said. "You mean blue and whites?"

"No! I do not mean policemen. I mean two people like us, who are leaving the casino when the man is arrested! You did not tell me this job was like this!"

She said, "Nothing like this ever happened to me before."

Like the man arrested in the casino, saying *There must be some mistake.* "Insurance," he said. "You did not say anything about terrorists, South African Catholics who think they are instruments of God!"

"La Mano de Diós," she said. "Were they from *La Mano de Diós?"*

"I do not know, they did not introduce themselves. I am not an assassin, I do not shoot people, do you understand? I do not know about security, I was a soldier, that was different! I was not even a very good soldier, just so-so. I do not know about politics! This is a mistake, I am not what you think I am!"

Max knocked, brought in tea. "Good night Ms. Ling."

"He should wait," David said. No sense sending the young man out alone. "Maybe people should wait until the police come."

"Max," she said, "someone approached David in the parking, threatened him. Maybe you better have people wait until the police get here, then someone will see you to transit or take you home, all right?"

Max looked at David. Angular face, skin the color of sandalwood and wiry hair that grew close to his head. A sleek young secretary with a job that might get him into the middle class. He didn't look frightened, just wary. It wasn't real for him. It wasn't real for Mayla, either.

"Make yourself a cup of tea, and don't let anyone else up or down the elevator until the police get here. They'll be able to access."

Max didn't want to leave, didn't want to stay. "Yes ma'am," he said finally. He closed the door softly, as if he might waken someone.

"I think I am not suited for this job," David said.

She did not answer.

"It was a period of probation," he insisted. "So I think I should go back." Meph, what to do about the kitten? Stupid to stay in a country because of a kitten.

"All right," she said. The color was bright in her cheeks. She is angry, he thought. But he didn't care.

"I need to hire someone else," she said, her voice low enough that it sounded in the upper registers of normal even in the air mix—or was he just getting accustomed to the way people talked? "I need to replace Tim, can you at least stay until then?"

"Tim can stay," he said harshly. Tim did not seem to want to leave. Tim would probably like all this macho shit about guns and terrorists.

"I really don't want Tim to stay," she said. She was not angry, she was embarrassed. The color in her face was embarrassment.

"What difference does it make, Tim or me?"

"There is a problem with Tim," she said. She wanted to avoid this.

"What?" he insisted, because he was angry and he wanted to push her.

She gestured to the air, not looking at him. "Tim and I, Tim thinks he is . . . that we are having a relationship. You see, I knew Tim before I hired him, we went out a couple of times."

Her discomfort was a palpable thing.

"It is my mistake, really," she said. "I should never have hired him. He said it was only for awhile, that he was going back to Australia. Now he says that he never said that. You see, he came back to Belize to clear up a problem I had with a bank suit, he did me a real favor. I feel like I owe him . . . something. But I'll talk to him, have him arrange the date to leave. Then you can leave. Only a couple of weeks, I promise."

"What about your insurance?" he said, goading her.

"Oh fuck the insurance! I don't care about the insurance. I'll tell them you quit unexpectedly and that I'm trying to replace you. It must happen. A few weeks," she said.

He shrugged.

"Please," she said—pleading like the woman in the parking—"don't mention quitting to Tim."

He wanted to laugh, he had already mentioned quitting to Tim.

But he felt tired, tired of these people and their wanting. It was easiest not to explain he had already said something to Tim. Easiest just to go along.

He sighed. "All right."

4

A Few Simple Things

At the police station, David was seated in front of a pale screen, empty of everything but light. Mayla closed her eyes and the afterimage of the pale screen was a red square. She could hear the hiss of the air-circulating system. "We will be monitoring your pulse rate, your eye movements and pupil contraction," the blue and white told David. "We will be showing you ims. If you can identify them, please name them for us."

"This is the same equipment that they use for interrogation?" David asked.

She flinched at the word "interrogation" but did not open her eyes.

The blue and white said, "You are not being interrogated, Mr. Dai."

"I understand," David said. "But these—" in his pause she imagined him searching for the English, "I was in the military, they use these things."

She thought of Tumipamba's white coffin and it was

there in her mind's eye, tilted up, with Tumipamba watching her from behind the glare of light on the glass. She couldn't get it out of her head so she opened her eyes. The screen was empty and bright, and Tumipamba's coffin was whited out.

People had sat in this room and been interrogated.

If it had been an interrogation, how would they make someone look at the screen? How would they keep someone's eyes open? Cut off their eyelids?

She blinked.

"Have you yourself ever been a subject before?" the blue and white asked David. "Conducted a session?"

David had not.

"Fine. Just relax. You won't feel any discomfort."

The first im was her own face in a less than flattering image. Oh God, it was from her driver's license.

"Mayla Ling," David said, "my employer."

Another im.

"Mr. Talsing, I worked for him in France."

Tim's. A woman he didn't know. Another woman. "Not familiar," David said.

Another woman.

"The President of France," he said, sounding amused.

Mayla let out her breath, not aware until that moment that she had been holding it.

A man.

"Familiar, but I cannot place him."

A square-faced oriental with deep lines around his mouth. "My father, Philippe Dai," he said so softly she leaned forward. Where did they get these images?

More people, some he knew, some he didn't.

Then they told him it was not necessary to talk although he could make any comments he chose. The system would measure the way he reacted and build off of the features he found familiar or resonant to construct her face. He should not try to picture the woman.

David frowned. "Do not picture her?"

"That's really a bit of a trick," the blue and white said, friendly. "It's like the old recipe to turn water into gold. Put it in a big pot on the back of the stove and stir it and stir it, all the time not thinking about a white rhinoceros. After I say it, all you can think of is the white rhino. Now eyes on the screen, Mr. Dai."

Ims began to flicker in front of him. Faces: some light, some dark, and most (but not all) female, shifting in a plastic blur, liquid chins and noses and cheeks and foreheads brightening and shading. They began to show certain characteristics: black eyes looked out, arrested, became fixed, while features shifted around them, melting and moving. Some alchemy measured the way David looked at things, how his pupils expanded, how his eyes moved when the face was familiar, what his heart did. *This* is familiar, their measurements told them, *that* is not.

Voudoun, she thought. Technological voodoo.

He started to turn his head and the blue and white said, "Eyes on the screen, Mr. Dai."

The features became less plastic, solidified. David was leaning away; in the light reflected from the screen she could see his shoulders and hands tense, pushing against the arms of the chair as if he were pushing up and back, over the back of the chair, getting away from the image in front of him. A woman's face was drawn out of him. Pulled out of him. It did not seem possible that they could do this. It did not seem right, or fair.

The ims flickered, slowed, stopped. There was a woman's thin black face with hard round apple cheeks and great dark eyes. David said, "It is the woman at the casino." He turned in his seat to look back at Mayla, "When we had dinner at Aphrodite."

The blue and white looked at her but she could only shake her head.

She couldn't remember the woman at all. Was the memory hiding somewhere in her unconscious? Could they

have pulled that face out of her, arising, all unknowing?
What else was down there that someone could pull out?

Stir and stir and stir, and at no time think of a white
rhinoceros.

They wanted David to register for a course in defensive
driving and a course on personal security. She wished he
could have stayed while she talked to the blue and whites
about what she should do now, but they wanted him to do
some ID for their records; retinal scans, DNA samples.

An officer, a blue and white with sergeant's bars on the
sleeves of her uniform told Mayla that she had to continue
with her life, that she must not allow terrorism to keep her
from functioning. The phrases the officer used were
phrases from the paper and the vid, so familiar that Mayla
heard them in capitals. "If you Allow yourself to Succumb
to Fear," the officer told her, "They have Succeeded. They
have Disrupted Society. The Only Way to Fight Terrorists
is make them Powerless."

On the other hand, she was supposed to take certain
precautions. She was supposed to do A Few Simple
Things. "Vary your schedule. Leave for work at different
times, change the route you take." She lived on a dead-end
street, she worked at the bank, no matter how she varied
her routine she had to start at the same place and end at
the same place.

There was a Delicate Balance between disruption and
Normal Common Sense. What, Mayla wondered, would
Abnormal Common Sense be?

"Who was the woman who approached David?" she
asked.

"Her name is Anna Eminike, she is wanted for a number
of charges both here and abroad. We are conducting an
investigation and we are closing in on these people. In the
meantime, just be a little careful."

Be a Little Careful, Mayla thought. "Is she part of *La
Mano de Diós*?"

The blue and white said, "I'm sorry, this matter is under investigation, that is not information I can give out."

"Why is she after me?"

"I'm sorry, Ms. Ling, but during an investigation we cannot talk about the particulars."

Had this woman singled her out because of the im in the newspaper? Or because they had seen her in the casino? But when they'd seen her in the casino, how did they find out who she was? David had told the blue and whites that the woman had said she was an instrument of God, that she was God's surgeon. Wasn't that what *La Mano de Diós* believed? That God told them what to do?

That there was providence in the fall of a sparrow? That God selected them to be the instrument of the sparrow's fall?

"Ms. Ling," the blue and white said, "your dossier indicates you travel quite a bit on business. It might be a good idea to go somewhere for a few days, perhaps the U.S. or Marincite?"

"Mayla," Polly Navarro said. "I'm sorry to hear about your trouble, but glad Marincite could help."

"It's actually a wonderful opportunity to work with your people on the MaTE restructuring," she said.

Polly's office was as formal as a royal court. The door was tall and wooden, like the doors of the Cathedral St. Nicolas. The whole right side of the office was virtual window. The scene was a city.

A secretary brought them coffee. He was a young man in a vanilla suit with amethyst cufflinks and buttons. He had amethyst slips in his eyes, too. He was absolutely silent, like a good waiter. Her coffee tasted like surface coffee. She glanced at the window again, not meaning to, and saw Polly follow her eyes. "Hong Kong?" she asked.

He nodded. "Hong Kong, 2038."

Okay. Although why he would want to look at Hong

Kong in that particular year eluded her. "Quite a display," she said.

"Thank you," he said. "I like it." He tapped a little brass control panel set in the desk. "Clear," he said, "orchids."

The window dimmed and came bright, and this time the wall looked into a greenhouse of orchids.

"Clear, Hokkaido." Twisted pine trees and mountains, mist and stone. At least they weren't as bright.

"Clear, Serengeti."

Desert at dusk and below them a muddy drinking hole.

"Impressive," she said. Voice activated. The money spent on this office would probably buy her a house.

"Set," he said. "I like the space in this one."

Lots of it, the plain falling away in a long sweep, darkening to blue in the dusk. Tim would like it, she thought, but it wasn't exactly her taste.

"I wonder if you would be willing to talk to someone here regarding a loan for a city project," Polly said.

For a moment she was surprised. Not that she should have been, deals usually required favors. "Certainly," she said. "Mr. Navarro, First Hawaiian would like very much to establish presence in Marincite in any way possible."

"I'll have him call you. Watch a minute," Polly said, "the lions will come down."

She looked at the window. And after a moment they came, bellies swaying and lean hips rocking, to crouch at Polly Navarro's waterhole and drink with long pink tongues.

Polly Navarro's "someone" came calling. Saad Shamsi was a gazelle-eyed Pakistani. "Just Saad," he said, and added, smiling, "rhymes with 'odd'." He was an aide with the Marincite City Department of Education and Health (he gave her his card). Aide could mean anything. His job may even have been a real job, although aide could mean anything.

He wanted a loan for a nursing school and clinic to be built in an area of town called, whimsically, Castle. "Are you familiar with Castle?" he asked, convincingly sincere. "It's not a very good part of the city. This way we can address two problems at the same time, the need to educate young people and provide jobs, and a way to increase health care."

Politician talk. She dropped the chip into her reader and looked at the figures. She could structure a loan proposal, it wasn't even a very complicated loan. "I don't foresee any problems," she said. There was no reason for Polly to send her this loan, it was a nothing loan.

There was nothing to be understood from Saad-rhymes-with-odd Shamsi, either. He was about her age. He spoke impeccable English, sounded North American rather than Caribbean. Maybe slightly British in his diction but it was hard to say. His suit was appropriate, that kind of neutral gold color that meant he could have bought the suit yesterday or five days ago. Not too expensive, so if he was skimming, he wasn't making big money, or at least not spending it on clothes. Not flashy.

"It looks straightforward," she said.

"Good," he said. "I mean, I didn't expect much problem."

"So why are you working with me?" she asked.

"What do you mean?"

She shrugged. "Anyone could do this loan."

"Mr. Navarro suggested you," Saad said. He was not evasive. He looked at her clear-eyed, his face open.

Maybe Polly really did just want to send some business First Hawaiian's way. This was a token, easy enough.

"Who knows why Mr. Navarro does anything," Saad said. "He sits in the middle of his web and pulls us all together." He shook his head. "Have you spent much time in Marincite?"

"Business trips," she said.

"Maybe I could take all of you around the city some evening?"

Then it will come, Mayla thought, whatever the secret cost of this loan would be. A loan for his mother at low interest. Financing something. "That would be wonderful," she said.

"Do you like jai alai?"

Tim loved jai alai. Terrific, Saad would get some tickets and they would go see some jai alai.

Saad Shamsi collected the three of them that evening after dinner. He didn't seem put off by having to take her security, seemed in fact to get on very well with Tim. He had tickets for good seats, although Mayla didn't know, she had never been to a jai alai match.

Jai alai players leaped, arms top-heavy with *cestas* like flamingo beaks whipping the ball. The games were fast, the slap of feet against the floor, an explosion and a yell. The odds changed constantly and she didn't understand the betting. A player leaped, flicking the ball across the court. His gear was brilliant red and he looked like a barbarian in armor covered at the vulnerable points: head, knees and elbows. He had silver streamers like tinsel tied around his biceps on his *cesta* arm. She wondered if that meant something, but not enough to ask.

It was hard to concentrate on the game. She didn't feel tired, not physically; fatigued, maybe. Eventually he would ask for it: a loan for a company run by a friend or that the administration of the monies for the construction work be handled by another company—selling the loan to him so he made half a percentage point a year.

If he'd just get it over with, then she could be done with this nonsense of jai alai and evenings of entertainment and get on with the MaTE loan. More meetings with Polly Navarro.

She wanted to see him again, wanted to talk to him, the way he had started to talk at the funeral. About terrorists.

About security. What would it be like to work for Polly Navarro?

The red player with the silver streamers scooped the ball, whirled and fired it, streamers tracing a fluid arc. Tim went to his feet, he had money on the game.

She felt out of touch. She thought of *La Mano de Diós* and suddenly she could not manage to care about the jai alai game or about Polly Navarro or MaTE.

She glanced to her left just as David looked her way and their eyes met. Nothing in his face. Her face felt the same way, nothing. They were just here, not part of this place at all, two people for whom the game and the excitement meant nothing. And then he quirked a tiny smile and shrugged ever so slightly, just a little gallic twist of his shoulders. "What can you say?" his shoulders said. And she felt herself smile back a bit.

"Secrets?" Saad said, catching her off guard.

He was watching her, too.

Tim looked down, puzzled, and in that moment something must have happened on the court because the crowd around them erupted. She stood up and cheered, too, sliding out from under Saad's gaze. The player in black and green walked to the side to pick up a towel and wipe his face—stage business that athletes use when they are in the spotlight. Off to the side stood the player in red, streamers hanging motionless. He looked bemused.

She knew how he felt.

Saad was back two days later to talk about the hospital and clinic loan. She had the loan of an office by then, and was started on the business of the MaTE deal.

"Hi," he said from the door, "just who you wanted to see, right?" She rolled her eyes in mock disgust and he came in and sat down. "Ms. Ling," he said, "my most favorite person in the whole world."

"Not because I'm going to give you a sizable chunk of money," she said.

"Of course not," he said.

His office had received quotes from construction firms and he had a change in some of the figures. She plugged the figures into the system. It wasn't a complicated loan at all.

Saad sat in a chair beside the desk, craning a bit to watch her. "Is that all?" he asked.

"That's it," she said.

"That's slap," he said. American slang, she knew it from the vid.

"What can I say?" she said.

"You're amazing," he said, mock serious.

"Your English is amazing."

He shrugged. Apparently he knew his English was good. It was casual and fast, and he always caught what she was saying. Bilingual. She wanted to know where he learned.

"I studied it at home, in Pakistan, and I lived in the U.S. for awhile," off hand, slightly embarrassed.

"Oh yeah?" she asked, "where did you live?"

"Cincinnati, Ohio," he said, and she laughed at the unexpectedness of it.

"That's funny?" he asked.

"Why Cincinnati, Ohio?"

"Actually," he said, "I lived in Los Angeles for a year, and then the company I worked for transferred me to Cincinnati. I liked Cincinnati." That sounded a little defensive. But he was smiling, he knew she had expected him to say someplace like New York or Miami.

"I'm sure it's a lovely town," she said.

"It is," he said, emphatic. "Believe it or not, I want to go back there. I want to go back to Cincinnati, Ohio, marry a blonde American girl, and have three perfect blonde daughters."

She shook her head. "Genetics are not on your side."

He sighed. "Biology is destiny, I know."

"So why did you leave?" she asked. "Did you get transferred here?" Marincite could have a subsidiary in Cincinnati, Ohio.

"No," he said, "the U.S. Immigration Department informed me that my presence in the U.S. was no longer an asset."

That surprised her, since he'd had a job.

"The U.S. says that you can't take jobs from American citizens. You have to be an engineer or a scientist or something, then they let you stay because there are never enough of those people. But not an administrator, a manager of a finance department." He looked down at his hands, now made pensive. She was sorry she had asked.

"Well," she said, "if those are the only changes to the loan you have, then we're still on our way. I'll have papers any time you want."

"I'll take them now," he said. "I can bring them back tomorrow with signatures."

She hadn't expected that, it was too easy. "You want them now?" she asked.

"Sure," he said. He sounded so American.

She printed them out and handed them to him. That was it? No catch? Saad Shamsi *was* odd if there wasn't a catch.

He looked through them and she felt her shoulders tense, waiting for him to say casually, "I have a friend. . . ."

"Looks good," he said.

"Do you foresee any problems?" she asked.

"What do you mean?" he asked.

"Getting signatures?"

He looked puzzled. "It's a pretty straightforward loan, isn't it?"

It was. Of course it was. Or would be in a place like the U.S. where people didn't pay each other to do business. "Unless someone wouldn't be in or something," she said.

"Oh," he said, "no, no problems. We've got a meeting tomorrow on the clinic so I can get this taken care of then.

If I can't get all the signatures tomorrow I can bring the papers back to you Friday, can't I?"

Of course he could.

That was it. All this time she had been waiting and that was it. The jai alai, reading motives into everything he did and said . . . he was just a nice guy. Oh, *Madre de Diós,* was she blushing? It wasn't her fault. It was the way business usually happened in Julia, she wasn't accustomed to Marincite. She had always heard Marincite was worse than Julia, but maybe that wasn't true at all, with the Uncles around keeping watch.

He stood up and buttoned his jacket. "Hey," he said.

"Hey," she echoed. "What?"

"Would you like to go to dinner with me, tonight?"

Would she like to go to dinner with Saad-rhymes-with-odd Shamsi? Well, sure. Why not? She hadn't been exactly fair to him. "Okay," she said. "That would be nice."

"Great," he said, "absolutely slap."

She laughed. What a decent, nice guy, she thought when he left. A date. How long had it been since she'd had a date? Months, maybe over a year. Not that she expected anything, she couldn't expect anything, he lived in Marincite and she lived in Julia and a relationship would be impossible over that distance. Besides, it was stupid to even start thinking about a relationship when he had just asked her for dinner.

It would solve all of her problems with Tim if she were dating. He would give up and leave. David wouldn't care, and he wanted to leave anyway.

Insane, all these thoughts running through her head, worrying about the equation of Saad, Tim and David. It was just a dinner date. Nothing more.

It would be wonderful to be out on a date.

Mayla was unprepared for how she felt when she saw him at the door to the suite. She smiled too much, she was too happy. "Hi, come in a moment." She wished this were over with, that this were the second or even the third time they were going out. It would all be easier then. "I'm sorry, David has to go with us," she said. Quickly, "He doesn't have to eat with us, just go—" Saad looked taken aback, "—because of the insurance and all of that."

"No problem," he said. Sweet relief.

Still awkward, though, to go out with Saad and have David in tow. She had never had to worry about that before because until she had been promoted she had never been required to have security. At least David wasn't Tim. David was quiet.

David stood just behind them on the people mover, his body angled away, watching the bright shops—in Central the lights were dimmed at second shift to simulate dusk.

She wished Saad Shamsi would take her hand. She wanted a hug. It was too soon, and if he had taken her hand then her longing would be destroyed because he would be forward, he would be pressuring her into an intimacy that didn't exist yet. He would destroy all trust. And besides, David was behind them, a chaperon carefully not watching them. She was too lonely, it was dangerous to go out to dinner with this man when she was so lonely.

She was thinking about what if something developed between her and Saad. She was thinking it was possible, he was in some ways so North American. Not a Caribbean male who would be threatened by her own success. And she liked him, he was funny and smart. She hadn't been fair to him at first. Some day she would tell him that. He would come to Julia some weekends and stay with her, she would come to Marincite some weekends and stay with him.

Maybe she would move to Marincite. She could imagine living here, and she could probably get a job with Marincite Corp.

She wondered what kind of family he had back in Pakistan. A gaggle of doe-eyed sisters in saris who spoke no

English? Was he a cultural stranger to his family? Were they cosmopolitan?

She knew they were just going out to dinner.

She wasn't really having these thoughts one at a time, they were kind of all jumbled up with standing here next to Saad, who was quiet because her bodyguard was standing behind them, pretending not to pay attention to them.

The restaurant was American. She wasn't really surprised.

"I will wait there," David pointed to a bench on the street. He showed her his book, something in French.

While they were waiting to be seated Saad said, "Isn't he allowed to eat?"

"He ate before we came," Mayla said.

Saad nodded.

"It's his job," she said.

"That's why there are two of them?" Saad said. "Days and evenings?"

"Well, no," she said. "Tim is quitting. David is taking over."

"Tim is getting a different job?"

"Tim isn't really security. It's complicated," she said. She wasn't going to explain Tim to Saad, certainly not now.

The dinner lurched along. They neither of them seemed to know how to conduct a conversation. It's a first date, Mayla thought. How could they save this? Through the menu bound in hunter green, and the too-expensive chowder and her glass of wine and his beer and crippling onward. He wasn't funny or quick and her head was empty.

It was her, he was usually different. Things had started wrong by having David come along. She should get things back to the way they had been in the afternoon when Saad had been easy to talk to but she didn't know how.

"Do you like Marincite?" she asked.

"It's all right," he said.

"It's not Cincinnati, Ohio," she said.

"No," he said. That was all, just "no." No quip.

"It's not like Julia, either," she said. "In some ways it's more like the U.S."

"How do you mean?"

"Well, it's sort of better organized. There's less bribery, maybe." Like you, she thought, although she didn't dare say it. He didn't understand, how could he? "In Julia, everything is paybacks and kickbacks and somebody has his hand in someone else's pocket. I know that happens in Marincite, too, but Marincite is different."

"I don't think Marincite is like the U.S."

"It's not, really," she said. "It's run by Marincite Corp., you're really not allowed to breathe without permission—"

"Air tax," he said, grinning. The old joke, in Caribe you even had to pay for the air you breathe.

"But Marincite keeps everybody running by company regulations, which is kind of honest. Julia's not like that."

"Sure," he said, although she couldn't tell if he really agreed with her or was just being agreeable.

"I was thinking of moving here," she said, "you know, getting a job with Marincite Corp." Which was stupid, because if she moved here, she would have to have a job with Marincite Corp. "I've been having some trouble in Julia, I've become a target of some, you know, political people."

"You?" Saad said. "I mean, not that you don't have a good job, but, I mean. . . ."

"I'm not important," she said. "Don't worry, I'm not insulted."

He grinned. "I mean, I think you're important, after all, you're doing this loan for me."

She felt her face crinkle with pleasure at his joke. "Well, my grandfather started First Hawaiian, that's the only angle that the police can come up with. But I guess that Marincite isn't really any safer than Julia. Look what happened to poor Tumipamba."

Saad had to think a second. "Oh, yeah. Right, the guy, the CFO."

She nodded. "If politicals could get to him. . . ."

"If it was politicals," Saad said.

"Yeah?" she said. "I heard something about gambling debts."

"I didn't hear that. But I think there's a shakedown going on at the upper levels of Marincite Corp."

"You think they're killing their own execs?"

"Hey," Saad said, "I don't know. And the walls have ears."

Another dead space. Too serious, she thought. She should have kept things light.

When dinner arrived she was grateful for the business of putting sour cream and butter on her potato. For the occupation of eating.

"I ah, I hate to bring up business at dinner," Saad said, "but I have a friend and he and I are trying to get something started and I was wondering if we might be able to talk to you about a loan?"

"A loan?"

He nodded.

"What kind of loan?" she asked, gone still inside. Suspended and waiting.

"For a business," he said. "I was wondering if maybe you could come with me and meet my friend, we could talk about it at the shop."

Not an answer, she thought, which was a different kind of answer. "Why don't we talk about this at the office tomorrow?"

"The shop isn't far," he said.

"I don't usually do business away from the office."

"We could get it over with."

"When?" she said. Maybe she wasn't being fair again. Maybe he would say Saturday or Monday, after the papers for the clinic loan would be signed.

"Tonight?" he was eager. "Would that be all right? It wouldn't take long."

No, she thought. No no no. "How about Friday?" she said. Hoping he would say "sure."

"Really," he said. "Tonight might be a better time."

"Or there might be trouble getting signatures on the loan papers?" she said. Rude, angry with him.

He didn't say anything, but it was true.

"Goddamn you," she said. And then, "Goddamn you, you have a lot of nerve."

"Yeah," he said. No explanation, no apology.

"Why did you wait until the night before the papers were signed!"

"Because the loan would almost be in your hand and it would be harder for you to say 'no'."

"What makes you think I need this loan? Do you have any idea how big a deal the Marincite loan is, and how really tiny your piddling clinic is?"

"It's all Marincite," he said. "This whole city is all Marincite."

Then she remembered that Polly Navarro had sent Saad.

She sighed. "Okay. Let's go see this friend."

There were lots of young people out on the street. She was glad of the noise, glad to have David behind her because it all kept Saad from saying much, just things like "cross here."

Mayla was so angry at herself. So stupid. All that fine speech about how Marincite was different. People don't borrow money from stupid bankers.

Saad took them down one of the hubs a couple of levels. "We have to take the chute," he said.

"Public transportation," Mayla explained to David.

The walkway back to the station was tiled in Marincite maroon and cream and they stood on the platform in silence. David looked at her, a silent question. "We're working," she said.

"Pardon me?"

"Bank business," she said.

Saad stared down the tunnel, at the concrete platform, anywhere but at her.

Served him right, she thought.

The chute was a string of seats, like an amusement park ride. Each pair of seats had a smoke-colored canopy. The one that came into the station was almost empty, only a woman with a string bag full of groceries near the front. Mayla waited until Saad started to climb in and then sat down in the seat behind him. David frowned but got in with her.

When the canopy came down the dome light came on. Saad glanced back, his face distorted by the plastic. She should have smiled but she looked down at her hands until the chute jerked forward. When she looked up it was at the back of Saad's head.

They went into the dark of the tunnel. In front of them was a string of dome lights, each made hazier by the succeeding layers of plastic canopies. The chute curved down.

"What is wrong?" David asked.

"Nothing," she said. "It's just business."

He looked at her a moment and then shrugged. "Okay."

"In my business," she said, "in this country, if you're going to do a loan for someone you have to do them a favor."

He smiled. "I think that when you get a loan, the bank does you a favor, no?"

"Maybe for regular people," she said. "Not for businesses."

"Ah," he said. "What kind of favor?"

"He wants a loan for a business he is starting up. Either it won't have any credit or it'll be illegal," she said.

"You do that?" he said, surprised. He regretted it. "I mean, it is not my affair."

"No," she said, "it is your affair, in a way. I mean, considering your job."

He didn't seem to care for that.

The string began to slow and curve upward and for a moment the dome lights in the front seemed to brighten as they curved above the canopy behind them. Then they leveled off. The dome light flicked out and David grabbed her arm, but then they came into the lighted station.

David laughed nervously, embarrassed.

The tile looked green and yellow through the plastic but when it lifted she could see that they were actually blue and white. Saad stood up, "This is our stop," he said.

On the wall it said "Cathedral."

One of the overheads was out at the exit and the tunnel beyond it looked dark. The tiles on the wall were cracked and scratched and painted with angry graffiti she couldn't read. David balked a moment, "Are you sure we are in the right place?"

"Why don't we do this in the office?" she said to Saad.

"We're almost there," he said. "You can meet my partner this way."

A few feet farther and the light was back, although dim. The tunnel smelled of urine and mildew. Then a flight of stairs and they were outside on the street. Mayla's shoulders were hunched and she had to make a conscious effort to loosen them.

There were lots of young people here in this hub, lots of couples. The kids were all dressed slap, some of the girls shining as if they were wet, looking like the pop singer, what-was-her-name, DanHe. David was tense, watching everything.

Saad seemed at home, although he was dressed too well to fit in. Following, watching the bare-armed boys standing corners, who were watching them, Mayla felt painfully obvious.

"It's not far," Saad said.

Two streets over and he stopped at a heavy, industrial

looking door and opened it with a key. They followed him up narrow, badly lit stairs to what looked like a manufacturing loft, mostly empty except for a couple of workbenches against the wall. At the end were a couple of offices, one with a light on.

Saad knocked on the door and then opened it without waiting. There were two people waiting. One was a young black girl, street pretty and feral, with a mane of tawny hair tipped in black. The other was an anglo, thick and middle-aged, with a moustache. "Saad," he said, "this is your banker?"

"Right," Saad said.

"Okay," Moustache said, "go get yourself a cup of coffee. *Café,*" to the girl, and then to Mayla, "decaffeinated?"

"No, thank you," she said.

"Antoinette will take care of Saad and your friend," Moustache said.

"No," Mayla said, "this is my security, he has to stay with me."

The girl took her feet off the desk and stood up. Moustache thought about it a moment and then shrugged. "Okay," he said. Then to the girl and Saad, *"Vamos."*

"I don't think—" Saad started.

"That's right," Moustache said, "you don't think. Go on."

Saad hesitated and the girl laughed, *"Viene chico."* Mayla didn't know if Saad understood Spanish or not, but he gave in and followed her out of the office.

"So you are a banker," Moustache said. "Pretty little blanc. What bank? The chico told me but I don't remember."

Moustache had brown hair and was fairer than she was—she thought he might be Argentine. "First Hawaiian," she said. David was behind her and she was glad he was there.

"Did the chico tell you about the business?" Moustache

gestured at the office. "It's a little manufacturing concern. We need some working capital to get started."

"What kind of manufacturing?" she asked. As if it mattered.

"Jewelry," he said.

Jewelry, she thought. Right. Who gave a damn about jewelry? "What just exactly is the problem?"

"Eh?" he said, frowning.

"With the loan," she said, impatient, wanting to be out of here. "What's the problem? Do you have a credit statement? Or is it *en la sombra*?"

Moustache flinched. Apparently anglo women bankers weren't supposed to say things like *en la sombra,* "in the dark." Or maybe he just didn't expect her to come out point blank and ask if it was illegal.

"There is a problem," he said in Spanish. There was always a problem. With papers, he explained. Her Spanish wasn't good but she could follow him well enough.

"¿Una problema con Los Tontons?" "A problem with the Uncles?" she asked. If Marine Security wasn't in on it she didn't want anything to do with it.

Oh, no no no, Moustache said, the Uncles were fine, everything had been arranged with the Uncles.

In English she said, "Do you have a front?"

"¿Qué?"

"A front," she said. "A business statement, balance sheet, for whatever this company is supposed to be. Something I can use as a credit statement at the bank."

"Ah!" Moustache understood, *"¡La barba!"* "The beard." *"Sí, yo lo tengo."* He had a chip and hard copy and passed it to her. The hard copy was the paperwork for a concern that made facsimiles of Incan and Aztec jewelry pieces using the lost wax technique. The facsimiles would be sold in the United States. Each piece would be made by hand.

She wondered what the business was. Caribe was an open gold market, like India, so there were no restrictions on buying and selling gold and the price wasn't regulated. Maybe fraud? Gold labeled fourteen carat when it was really eight? Or the pieces would be sold as the actual items rather than reproductions? Or maybe nothing connected to jewelry at all.

"How much?" she asked.

"200,000cr," he said and started to say more but Saad was in the door. "What is it?" he said, brusque.

"Nothing," Saad said. "I'm just your partner, remember?"

"You have done your part," Moustache said. "Now let me do mine."

"I'm not going to say anything, I'm just going to listen, okay?"

"I tell you everything."

"So if I'm here, then you don't have to tell me."

Moustache was irritated. Mayla glanced back at David, he looked very tense. "Okay," Moustache said to Mayla, "this is how the money will be handled."

He wanted the money to come through a numbered credit account, and the mailing address to be a mail drop. Two-bit, crooked little game, she thought. What was she doing here? She didn't handle legitimate loans this small. She didn't like Moustache, she was royally sick of Saad-rhymes-with-odd Shamsi. And she was offended.

Bankers were not supposed to be offendable. The credit committee wouldn't have any trouble with this, as long as the credit statement checked out—and she knew it would. With the papers for the front, the bank could pretend ignorance in the event something happened, could even claim fraud.

"I have to put this through the credit committee," she said. "I won't know until the bank approves it. But it should be fine."

"Excellent," Moustache said. "Thank you for coming. If you need to get in touch with me, you may do so through Saad."

She didn't have any intention of getting in touch with him. She had done some strange things to get loans, but she had never sat in a manufacturing loft in the wrong part of town. If Saad had wanted to buy the loan that would have been fine. People did that. People came to her office. But this was two-bit, shoddy, appalling.

The girl was sitting on one of the bare work tables in the loft, swinging her legs. She was dressed like a pop vid star; lynx-haired, black industrial nonskid top, rainproof boots. Too much makeup. Not much jewelry, though, just a plain bracelet. She was leaning back on her arms and the bracelet was turned around so the flat black plate was pressed against the inside of her wrist. The bracelet struck Mayla as odd, but she wasn't up on industrial chic. The girl looked at Mayla, looked down at her own wrist and laughed. *"Un otra pollo,"* she said to Moustache. "Another chicken."

"Shut up," Moustache said.

"Hasta luego, hermana," the girl said, "See you later, sister," and laughed again.

"Yo no soy tu hermana," Mayla said. "I'm not your sister."

"Va a la oficina," Moustache said, the way someone would tell a child to go to their room, but the girl didn't move. She was still sitting on the table, watching them, while Mayla promised she would get back to Saad when she had heard from the credit committee.

Saad took them down to the street. "Go straight for three blocks, then turn left." He pointed, not looking at her. "That'll take you to the chute." At least he had the decency to be embarrassed.

David was still, looking up and down the street.

The boys were still on the corner, watching, and there was a swirl of Indian dance music from the Indian restaurant across from them, light spilling through the beaded doorway. A little street cleaner swished up the street, leaving a black trail that reflected the overhead lights.

"The girl," David said, "she was wearing a bracelet, how do you say it, retro-action, ah, you know, stimulation neural." His inflection was French.

For a moment it didn't mean anything to her. Stimulation neural, neural stimulation. Then it did. A self-stimulating system, a neuro-feedback bracelet. It set up feedback to stimulate the wearer's own nervous system, banish fatigue, increase awareness and induce a mild state of euphoria.

A goddamned slave bracelet.

That was the jewelry business, making slave bracelets. Extremely addicting. "Christ," Mayla said. "You're sure?" But as soon as she understood him she knew it was true.

"I have never seen one before, except on the vid," David said. "Maybe that is not what it is."

"Did you understand what they wanted?" Mayla said.

"They want money, for this business, yes?"

Yes. Oh yes. Oh Christ. Oh *Madre de Diós.* It wasn't illegal for her to cut the loan because they had never told her what they were going to do. And their papers would check out. Oh, sure, they would check out.

"What are you going to do?" David asked.

"I don't know," she said.

"Ah," David said. Nothing else, just "ah." As if she had told him something.

The beads clattered across the street and out of the restaurant came two boys and a girl, her bright hair burgundy under the light. She was stumbling and the boys had hold of her arms. They were laughing and she was laughing, but hers was a high, nervous laugh, the sound of a drunk who didn't quite know what the joke was.

"You're okay," one of the boys said, a delicate-looking Indian boy whose bare arms were smooth and muscled.

"I'm fine," she said.

"Oh yeah," the other boy said. "You're *fine.* Come on."

"I have to go home now," she said. "I have to go

home." The boys were laughing. She flicked her hair back and the red dot of her caste mark stood like a stigmata on her forehead, the color of her dyed hair. "I have to go home now," she said helplessly.

"You're okay," the first boy said, looking over her at the other boy.

The boys on the corner were still watching Mayla and David. But then an intoxicated girl wouldn't be very interesting to them.

David was waiting, his face neutral, the way it had been in the jai alai game. What did all this look like to him? Down here in the wrong part of Marincite, making loan deals with people who fabricated illegal neural-stimulation devices.

She had never done anything like this in her life.

"We should not stay here," David said quietly.

Her boots were meant to be worn to a nice restaurant, not for the streets of Cathedral in Marincite. They clicked as she walked. David's sandals were noiseless. David was mostly noiseless. Carefully unobtrusive.

"The boys are walking behind us," he said, *sotto voce*. "Do not turn around. I think they are just bored."

"Okay," she said, but her voice was too small for him to hear. Not that it mattered. Click click click click. Her boots were so damned loud. A target. Why hadn't Saad arranged the loan in her office? An amateur. It was all just too wrong. Slave bracelets.

What was she doing here?

In thirty minutes she would be back at her room, and this would all be over.

She wanted to go home. She wanted to sleep in her own bed. She was afraid of this place. She hated Marincite.

It was a longer walk than the way they had come, but at least they didn't have to go through the tunnel the way they had come out.

"Are they still following us?" she asked.

"I do not think so," David said. "I think, you know, they are just bored."

White tile on the walls with blue letters—Cathedral.

What the hell was she doing here? It's your job, she thought. She didn't want to get pulled into this. What if they wanted more? The bank would love it, a foothold in Marincite. As long as they could keep their paperwork clean. But she didn't want it, didn't want Saad Shamsi or Moustache in her office. It was too easy to imagine, a couple of years from now, being in bed with these people. If she continued in A&M, if she kept getting larger loans, what kind of people was she going to get into bed with?

Danny Tumipamba in his coffin. Who had he been in bed with?

"It isn't worth it," she said. And as soon as she did she felt a faint trembling through the soles of her feet. The chute coming to take her out of here. A sign, a portent, a reward from on high. God played dice with the universe, generating random numbers, or maybe only almost random numbers.

David looked at her, curious.

"I'm not doing the loan," she said.

"Ah," he said, not surprised.

"What kind of problems?" Saad said. "With the paperwork? I can call someone, get it cleaned up, whatever it is."

"No," Mayla said. "It's not that. I just think you need another banker."

"What's the problem?"

You lie down with dogs, you get up with fleas, she thought. And yet, she could make up a problem, something small, and he could go off and get it fixed up and then she would make the two loans, Moustache's and the clinic.

"You think it won't pan out? It'll be fine," Saad said. "The bank is clean."

"I don't like your business partner," Mayla said.

"And what is that supposed to mean?" He sat down in a chair, his knees wide. "It's some kind of popularity contest? He has the strings and the expertise. You think I know anything about manufacturing that stuff?"

"How did you get into this?"

"Everyone has a racket in this city. Everyone."

"So you had to have one, too," she said. "Don't you realize that once you get into bed with these people they mark you? You never get out again?"

"Wrong," he said. "One time is all I need. Three million in U.S. dollars. Then I qualify for resident alien status."

"Oh, right," she said. "A blonde wife and three blonde daughters in Cincinnati, Ohio."

"That was a joke," he said.

"Well, I'm not going to emigrate to Cincinnati, Ohio, Saad. This is my home. And I don't have any desire to crawl between the sheets with your partner."

"So you're clean," he said. "Everything you've ever done is clean."

"What difference does it make," she said. "Whether I'm clean or not, right now I'm telling you to find another banker."

He ran his hands over his hair. "Okay," he said.

She waited for him to say more.

"What else do you want me to do?" he said. "If you won't touch the deal, you won't touch the deal. I'll take my clinic loan to someone else. Someone in Marincite."

She wanted to go home. The longing for her own house, her own kitchen and living room and bedroom, drowned her, and then washed off her. Time to go home, she thought.

"I'm sorry," she said. "I hope you get to Cincinnati."

He looked at her, a gazelle-eyed Pakistani, Saad-rhymes-with-odd. "Polly Navarro will hear about this," he said.

The MaTE loan was big, too big for Polly to jeopardize it for something like this, wasn't it?

"Let me think about it and get back to you," she said.

"Don't take too long," he said.

The secretary ushered her in to Polly's office. This time the suit was cinnamon and the cuffs and slips in his eyes were tourmaline green. Polly had his back to her, working at a console, and he glanced back over his shoulder, his face flat.

"I'm sorry to bother you," she said.

He didn't let her off the hook, didn't say it was all right, just wheeled his chair around.

"I need to get back to Julia," she said. Work piling up there, and she needed some of the bank's resources to work on the MaTE loan, too.

Hong Kong was out the window. If it had been the lions coming down to drink then she would have been worried, but didn't Hong Kong just mean "Business is business"? She waited for him to bring it up, obliquely. Something about how were her other leads in the city going, or was First Hawaiian picking up some business in Marincite.

"We'll see you soon, then," Polly said.

It would be all right when she got home. Things would be normal.

So she went back to work. Up the elevator, gray, bone and red tweed reflecting in the polished elevator door. She ran the paperwork through for the renewal of a note for Asset Corp., talked on the phone about the possibility of upping a line of credit and ran it through to see what the credit committee would think of the numbers. With one thing and another she was there until after six, and when she came down the hall she saw David sitting in reception, reading.

He stood up as she came down the hall, sticking one thumb in his book to mark the page.

"Good evening, David."

"Good evening, Mayla."

Max was gone for the evening, but the elevator recognized David so he palmed it and they waited. So ordinary. Into the elevator.

"I'll get the car," he said when the door opened.

She didn't want to wait so she said, "Don't bother."

"Busy this afternoon?" he asked.

"Not so bad—"

He shoved her behind one of the concrete supports. She hit it with both palms, holding it and he kept pushing, pushing her down. She didn't even realize she'd heard the shot. In fact, what she heard first was the shattering of the back window of the car behind them and she thought—there's a bomb in the car.

Everything was so normal and she had the insane desire to ignore it, to step backwards, into normality.

The heel of her hand scraped along concrete, the air tasted of dry concrete dust. His hand was between her shoulder blades, holding her down. He sprinted to the next pillar, his run liquid if uneven with his bad knee, and she could still feel his hand between her shoulder blades, although when she concentrated she could feel that it was gone, that her skin just remembered it. Time to think of all this, but outside of time. She watched him flatten against the concrete support, he had a gun, where had he been wearing the gun?

He held the gun out, aimed, it jumped twice, and then he dropped but did not fall. Afterwards she could not remember hearing the sound of those two shots. It must have shattered that concrete garage, echoed. An engine hummed, whined into high gear, she heard that. The headlights flashed across the wall and towards the exit. The car was gone.

Then she ground her teeth. She could make a noise and she tried, and for a moment nothing would come, but then she managed, "David?" And she was back into time. Then she was afraid.

David stood from his crouch, unhurt. Until he stood up

it hadn't occurred to her that he might be. He came back, looking over his shoulder, around the garage.

"You are all right," he said.

"Yes," she said clearly, and then realized that she was, and that this had happened to her. She didn't know what it meant that it had happened to her. "Yes, I am."

He stood and looked at where the car had disappeared.

"Are you?" she asked.

"What?"

Every sentence hung in the air, unconnected to the others. "Are you all right?"

"Yes," he said, standing above her, tension making him all cord and wire. His eyes followed the walls of the garage all the way around and if she tried it was as if she could see where he was looking. He held the gun pointed up and away in a manner that made her think he knew how to use a gun, the way cops do on the vid. Then he looked down and frowned and helped her up, looked at her hand where she had scraped it. His fingers were cool, cradling her hand.

"I didn't do anything," she said, apologizing. "I just sat there."

"You did fine," he soothed.

"I didn't even know what was going on."

"Nobody does the first time." He smiled. "It is like sex. But it is all right now." Still watching he put his hand in the small of her back—like we're dancing, she thought— and walked her to the car.

"Looks like you're earning your keep," she said, trying to joke. Grace under pressure and all that.

He opened her door. "I did not do right," he said.

"You did fine," she said.

He slammed the car door, surely that was not as loud as those two shots, but she couldn't find them in her memory. "I did not go get the car," he said. "I should get the car, not walk with you."

"I told you to do that. I did that, and I didn't do anything at all when they were shooting. They could have done anything." They could have killed her, the stupid bystander in the background of the im, the one with her mouth open, not running, not ducking, just standing there, the one that she always looked at and thought, "I wouldn't be like that."

"Mayla," he said, "you aren't supposed to do anything except stay out of the way." He put the car in gear.

"Oh God," she said.

He put the car back in park and leaned across the gearstick. "It's all right," he said, putting his arm around her shoulders. His shoulder, even leaning across the gearstick, was bony and solid. "It's over." She wanted to be reassured.

His heart was beating, she could hear it with her ear against him. "You're scared, too." That was a relief, maybe she could learn how to know what to do even when she was scared, although she hadn't been scared, she hadn't been anything.

Anna Eminike did this, all the time. What kind of person would have a life like this? What kind of person would willingly be this afraid?

Anna Eminike was probably in that car. She felt sick.

"Don't worry," he said, "we'll go to the police."

She wanted to say that nothing like this had ever happened to her, she wanted to protest the outrage. It sounded so banal she didn't say anything.

5

Mephistofeles

The police station was as cold inside as it was outside on the street—but every place in Caribe was cold, David just always expected it to be warmer. At the high front desk the uniformed sergeant was talking to another officer in tan and the console was chiming a call. The sergeant gestured as he talked, "I've got five people on it already, but they're telling me to send another team out, what am I supposed to do?"

"I hate that son of a bitch, Claude," the uniformed officer said, "I told you, I don't want to work under him."

The sergeant raised his voice over the chirp of the console. "I know, I know, but if I don't send you out, Mardalin will."

Goddamn frigging third-world country, David thought. He was still full of the anger that came with adrenaline.

"What am I supposed to say?" Mayla asked softly.

"Tell him there was a shooting," David said.

"It sounds like we fell out over a pachinko debt or something." Her voice quivered on the edge of control. He thought about putting his arm around her but that would probably start her crying. He wished the sergeant would answer the call.

"I'll explain," he said.

She shook her head. "I should."

Maybe it made her feel more in control. She stood at the front of the desk until the sergeant waved off the man in tan. "Officer," she said, "My name is Mayla Ling, I'm an executive with First Hawaiian, and someone just shot at me."

"I'm sorry," he said, over the insistent call, "What did you say your name was?"

"Mayla Ling."

David wondered if the call was an emergency. Why didn't they have someone else answer?

"Can you spell it for me? Last name first." He keyed her name into his console and picked up the call while he rifled through screens.

"He's checking my credit record," Mayla said. David smiled back. She was trying. His smile was a crocodile smile to hide his anger.

One of the walls was broken as if it had been kicked in and there was a piece of plastic and some tools on the floor. The color scheme was a kind of grimy institutional rose. He'd seen army bases in Africa that looked better than this. The sergeant transferred the call.

"Ms. Ling," the desk officer said, "Someone will be out in a moment."

No maintenance. No sense of urgency. They stood. David's knee ached. A shooting, he thought, and these people are unconcerned. Terrorists were shooting at people, and he and Mayla were waiting, as if they were at the doctor's office or something. Too much violence, these people were so jaded by violence they didn't even respond. Like Africa, this rundown police station and the feeling that there was too little money and no energy.

It was fifteen minutes before a woman in street clothes came out and introduced herself as Sergeant Andre-Baptiste. She took them down a hall lined with old plastic filing cabinets, then through a maze of cubicles. The big room full of cubicles was the same dirty rose as the front. Most of the desks were dark. Well, it was after six. David counted aisles, they turned right at the fourth and hers was the first cubicle. Her name-sign was stuck on top of the chest-high wall of the cubicle. The 'p' in Andre-Baptiste was missing.

She didn't look Haitian, even if she had a Haitian name; her hair was fine, pale brown, crinkly, and her skin was the color of her hair. Her eyes were spaced too wide. She motioned towards the chair by the desk and Mayla hesitated, then sat down. Sergeant Andre-Baptiste flicked through screens and said (apparently to the screen), "This interview is being recorded, do you understand that a rec is being made of everything you say? Please answer vocally."

"Yes," Mayla said.

"You just had an incident, didn't you?"

Incident?

"Yes," Mayla said, "two people approached David in the parking at work, what, a week ago?"

Ah, an "incident" was something reported to the police. Was a shooting an "incident" or was there some sort of scale? Maybe it was an "occurrence"?

The sergeant looked up. "You're Jean David Dai?"

"Yes ma'am."

In island-accented French she asked. "How do you like Caribe?"

"It's all right." For Mayla's benefit he added in English, "But cold."

"Do you speak French?" the sergeant asked Mayla.

Mayla shook her head.

"I was just asking your bodyguard how he liked it here."

"Your family is Haitian?" Mayla asked, her voice polite, faintly artificial.

He looked around the cubicle as they talked, wishing he could sit down. Caribe, it was insane. Except he thought insane was actually a legal description that meant unable to distinguish between right and wrong. It was possible to be quite crazy and still know that what you were doing was wrong. As a diseased society, did Caribe know it was wrong?

Were they going to do that business of identification, as they had done with the woman? He hoped not, he had not seen anyone. It made him uncomfortable to have reactions he could not control tapped. It was strange, to sit there and watch that face form. A kind of theft. Was it the !Kung, the bushmen of Africa, who had once believed that taking an im would steal the subject's soul?

Africa. He wasn't going to think about Africa. This was not Africa, this was Caribe, and he was going to go home in a few weeks.

"Can you tell me what happened?" Sergeant Andre-Baptiste asked Mayla.

"David saw more than I did," Mayla said. "I cowered."

"That's good, people who cower live longer. I'll ask Mr. Dai what he remembers but I need your answer, too."

She should separate us, David thought. Compare our answers and see how our stories are different: not let us prompt each other, not let me tailor my story to fit Mayla's. Basic military procedure with disciplinary and criminal matters and prisoners of war.

"I don't remember anything, really," Mayla said. "I got off work and went down to the parking—"

"What time did you leave work?"

"A little after six?" She looked at him to confirm. He kept his face blank and waited for the sergeant to say that she wanted Mayla's estimation, but she didn't. She just typed two-fingered and they waited for her.

"Sergeant," he said, "are you going to send someone to the parking?"

The sergeant shrugged. "They're gone now, I'll send someone down but they won't find anything."

"Someone tried to shoot Ms. Ling," David said.

"Probably *La Mano de Diós*," she said conversationally. Of course, it's just a terrorist organization, he thought. These people! "So," she continued, "you finished work at a little after six, is that the time that you usually leave?"

"Sometimes, sometimes earlier, sometimes I work late. I don't really work an eight-to-five job, and you, I mean the police told me to vary my schedule so I have been."

"Wait," David said. "What are you going to do? I should not be here while you have her, what do you call it, *deposition*."

"You're not being accused of anything," the sergeant said.

"But it will not be clean," David said. "I will hear her story."

Sergeant Andre-Baptiste frowned. "I'm aware of procedure. I don't think that kind of formality is necessary under the circumstances."

"You are not sending anyone down there. These are terrorists."

"Mr. Dai," the sergeant said, "I know these are terrorists, and you are frightened but this day the Deputy Minister of Finance's home was blown up and eleven people died. This department is strained trying to deal with that. You were not hurt so they intend to frighten you, not to kill, or you would both be dead. If I made a fuss every time some group decided to harass an executive I would tie up this entire police force and that would be doing exactly what these people want."

"So you treat this as if it were adolescents drinking, or a skid stopping traffic?" David asked. He would start to shake. He always did this, after he got angry would come the shakes.

"We will check it out and make a note in the file," she

said, coolly. "If you are contacted by this group, please, you tell us."

"Third-world country, third-world police force," he said in French.

The sergeant looked at him for a moment. "Mr Dai," she said in English, "if you want to get a cup of coffee, or use the restroom, they are that way," she nodded her head towards the hall. "You take a little walk and come back when you feel better. Now, Ms. Ling, how many ways are there to get from your office to the parking?"

David stalked down the hall until he found a machine that dispensed lukewarm Caribe coffee.

In the morning David had a vague sense of being hung over, a metallic taste in his mouth, a fatigue almost like an ache in all his joints.

"Are you still quitting?" Tim asked. He was at the end of the hall, filling up the opening to the living room.

It was early in the morning, too early to deal with Tim. David shrugged. "Why?"

"Well," Tim said, "someone ought to, you know, be taking care of things, since I'm leaving and you're quitting."

"Maybe a professional," David said. "Excuse me, I need a coffee mug."

"I was thinking," Tim said, "you sounded pretty professional back there. Why don't you stay for awhile?"

"I am not the person for this job," David said. "Excuse me."

Tim stepped back but followed him into the kitchen. Coffee was made, that meant Mayla was up. He wondered if she wanted to go to work at the regular time.

"Don't you feel bad about leaving her like this?" Tim asked. "What if something happens?"

"Something has already happened," David said.

"Yeah," Tim said, "something has happened. And you and I are running out on it."

David shook his head, poured his coffee.

"Don't you feel any obligation?"

"I cannot stay here," David said. "Do you understand? I have done what I could do, in Africa. I have already paid."

He would have to buy a coffee mug, even if he was only going to be here for a few more weeks. Maybe he could just forget to bring this one back.

Tim was standing there still, watching. Or thinking, David wasn't sure which. *Obligation.* There was no *obligation.*

"You shot at the car," Tim said.

Shot at the car? Ah, in the parking. "Yes?"

"What were you trying to do?" Tim said. "I mean, were you trying to shoot the people or disable the car?"

What was he trying to do? He had to stop, think a minute. When he shot at the car, what had he been aiming at? Just the car. So why shoot at the car? If he had somehow stopped it, then he might have had to worry about the people in the car getting out and shooting at him. And he hadn't really thought about the people in the car.

"I was just shooting," David said. "They shoot at me. I shoot back so they will leave so we can escape." To be honest, he had not thought anything. He had just shot, because he was being shot at and he had a gun. He had not even thought about firing in a concrete parking, about ricochets or wild shots or how crazy this all was.

"I've never shot a gun," Tim said. "Except on a range."

Tim was still watching him. Like he was crazy? No, maybe with a funny kind of respect. Stupid, just because he had shot a gun at some people. People did not understand. Tim did not understand. Any thickheaded idiot can walk into a liquor store and shoot at someone. "That's good," David said. "I hope you never do shoot one. I wish I never had."

* * *

There was no one in the parking that morning. Or the next morning.

Saturday he wondered how he was going to fill the day. Maybe Mayla would need errands done or would want to go see her grandfather. He wondered what her grandfather thought of the shooting. Old man in his chair, sitting there like a relic of colonialism.

The cat got out when he opened the door to go get his coffee. Getting out was the reason for Meph's existence. He chased the kitten down the hall and it went under the couch in the living room. Mayla was looking up as David came by the kitchen. "I am sorry," he said. "He is like a child, you know?"

She laughed. "Let him roam around a bit, he won't hurt anything."

"I can get his food, he always will come for food."

"Get your coffee first," Mayla said.

Saturday morning, she was in a sweater and tights. The casual Mayla. Easier to be around, not so serious as when she was a banker. At the bank, Mr. Morel's driver Luis called her "Princess Ling."

He poured coffee. "Did you get the paper?" he asked.

"The *Journal*," she said. She got two papers, a financial paper from New York and a local paper.

"I'll see if the other is in," he said.

"Don't bother, it's all fiction," she said. She didn't like the Julian paper, she always said it was third rate.

"I would miss my serials," David said.

She shook her head. "How can you read those things?"

"They are easy, even for someone with my English."

"Written for people with the reading skills of ten-year-olds."

David nodded. "Yes, like me."

She laughed.

The paper came with the mail, in the living room near the garage door. Meph followed him. Julian mail was delivered by forced air. There were a couple of letter cans

and a cylinder and the paper. David picked up the paper.
Trouble in the Colombian Republic (underneath the headline in smaller print, "American Support Insufficient to
Buoy Unpopular Regime"). He stopped, looking at the
headline rather than the cylinder, ready to scoop it up, and
glanced down at the address. The address read Ms. M. K.
Ling. He stopped, hand still out.

He stood someplace else in his experience, looking at the
cylinder. It was about the length of his hand from the tip of
his longest finger to the heel. The front was dirty translu-
cent plastic, filled with oily liquid. The base was a pressure
trigger for explosives, a dull beige disc that was sensitive to
vibration. There was a bomb in Mayla's house.

The bomb must have been dropped nose first into a
mailing chute so the pressure-sensitive trigger would be
spared the slight stresses of acceleration and friction. That
could have been done anywhere; on the mall, in the mail-
chute at the end of the street. The air in the chute would
catch it and cushion it; maybe it was tampered with so it
would not be so sensitive, to insure that the steady acceleration would not disturb the trigger and that was why it had
not gone off when it landed in Mayla's living room. Or
maybe it had just managed to land in the way that would
not set it off. Maybe it was dead, a dud, or meant to scare.
Maybe it wasn't. If it wasn't, and it went off, besides killing
whoever was standing close by, it would breach the integrity of the dome. The dome would implode around them.
They would be dead before they knew it.

Except of course, himself, he would be dead but he knew
it already.

He couldn't do anything about the bomb, he didn't
know if the trigger was working or not and if it was and he
touched it he could set it off. If it was unstable from tam-
pering it might just go off by itself. So he must do something about his people.

Time was moving so slow, blue time they called it during
the war. He thought all these things in the time it took him

to read the cylinder, then straighten, unconsciously hiking his shoulder to keep a nonexistent rifle strap from sliding.

"Tim, Mayla," he called.

"What?" Tim called down from the loft.

"Listen to me. There is a bomb in the mail." He didn't know any other way to say it.

"What?" Tim said, "What the hell?"

"Did you call?" Mayla asked from the kitchen. She came to the door with a cup in her hand.

"I said," he was talking to his people, he must impress them, move them with his voice, "there is a bomb in the mail. Now you must leave."

"David—" she said.

"Now!" he snapped.

"Did you say a bomb?" Tim said.

"Wait on the street, walk softly. Go on." He was standing as still as he could.

"Can you do something," Tim asked, "can someone defuse it?"

"I am doing something. This is not the vid. Go on. Walk softly, it may have sensitive."

Mayla did not believe, he could see. It was not doubt, she just did not comprehend. She stood in the kitchen entrance, still holding her coffee cup. "My things," she said.

He shook his head. "Come on, Mayla," he coaxed. "We must leave or perhaps we will all die."

She looked at the cylinder, then came towards him, putting her feet down carefully, as if they were sore. She was wearing sandals. She had long feet. Gingerly, she opened the door to the garage. For a moment she looked at the button to open the big, outer garage door and he knew what she was thinking, it might set the bomb off. She looked at him. Tim, standing and waiting for Mayla to go first, looked at him. He shrugged, it was the way out. So she tapped it and the door went up smoothly.

"Son of a bitch," Tim breathed.

"Okay," he said, and she went down the curving steps.

Tim walked with his eyes on the floor as if walking a line. Like a drunk walking for a policeman. He stopped and looked at the cylinder for a moment. Then back at David. He did not believe, David thought. Not really. In his head he understood, but he did not believe.

"Go on," David said.

Tim shook his head.

David followed him onto the steps. He looked back at Mayla's pretty house. The kitten was at the mail, sniffing the edge of a capsule.

"Mephisto, non!"

The kitten looked up and his tail twitched.

"Venite! Maintenant!" he called the kitten.

"What are you doing?" Tim looked up the curve of the stairs down into the garage. Blue eyes.

"Calling the cat," David said, "go on."

"Fuck the cat," Tim said.

He should, he knew. Mephisto decided to go back towards his rooms. Little cat, he would never see the sun.

"Mephistofeles! Venite," he called. Insolent, the kitten walked to the hall. He could go to the kitchen and get out a food packet. Sifting through the rubble of the dome, he thought, police find his remains clutching a cat-food packet. He followed the kitten back across the living room, walking carefully, feet falling smoothly, rolling to minimize his weight although it probably didn't make any difference. The big orange and yellow sun beamed benevolently, oblivious to the black water. It was a tiny warmth; it, Mephisto, himself, they would be smothered, extinguished in an instant. If the trigger was still active. If the bomb would still go off. The cat disappeared into his bedroom. He remembered when he had first been in Afrique, a corporal had carried a dead shell as a good luck piece. They'd all been told not to pick up anything, but they did. One time, the corporal had taken it out of his pocket and left it sitting on the tailgate of a transport and it had rolled off and exploded. All the time the corporal had carried it in

his pocket nothing had happened and then, at that moment, it fell and went off. Or maybe it did not, maybe the corporal had carried his all through the war and that was a story he had heard and gotten confused. He'd seen a shell go off but he couldn't remember when.

The shoulder patch of an American Air Force Observer had a sword through a heart and emblazoned underneath it the word "DILLIGAFF." He said it meant "Do I Look Like I Give a Flying Fuck?" Funny thing to think of.

Half crouched, David stalked the cat down the hallway.

In the bedroom the kitten watched over its shoulder and when it saw David it flattened its ears and went under the bed. He crouched by the edge and it slunk out of reach. David clucked his tongue against the roof of his mouth. The kitten hissed, back against the bottom of the bed.

Don't be stupid. Leave him.

"David!" Tim must be standing at the top of the stairs.

He lay down, chest against the rug, and reached under the bed. His hand fell short. *"Mephisto, Mephistofeles, venite."* The bomb was going to go off, the water was going to come in and the cat was going to get them both killed. He reached again, Meph lashed out and scratched the back of his hand. The cat was panicked. He should go now. He reached again, palm up. Meph lashed again and he caught the cat's paw. Meph reflexively sank his claws into the meaty base of David's thumb. David hauled on the kitten who squalled in terror and anger and tried to dig claws into the rug. He yanked the kitten out, Meph grabbed his shoulder, still screaming.

"Jesus fucking Christ!" Tim said, watching him come down the hall. In the living room he thought it felt colder. Of course that was crazy, the room wouldn't be colder until the water came in and then it would be very cold.

He limped down the steps, counting them, the cat craning around to see the garage. At the base of the steps he palmed the door latch and the big safety door creaked and closed off Mayla's house as he watched. It would have to be opened by the security company now that it had been manually closed. It probably wouldn't stop the water from coming into the garage. He looked at the Skate. There was a lot of money in that car. He wondered if it should be moved, but hell, the insurance would pay for it. He shifted Meph to one arm and sprinted the last distance. Tim palmed the big watertight garage doors and they slammed into place, powered by the water force they were built to withstand. David winced, expecting explosion.

But there was nothing.

He looked at Mayla and Tim and grinned. Adrenaline made him suddenly, furiously happy.

"What the bloody hell were you doing?" Tim asked.

"He wanted to play with it. I thought maybe he would explode it before we were outside. We should call the police." He put his arm around Mayla's shoulders and squeezed. She was still holding her coffee cup.

"What kind of bomb is it?" she asked.

"Not a very good one," he said. "We should go and call the police. I can explain to everyone once."

They walked to the next house. David kept his arm around her shoulders and did not allow her to look back. He kept expecting the explosion behind him, kept waiting for it to go off, knowing it would startle him. Each minute it didn't go off made him think that maybe it wouldn't; that Mayla's house, the yellow sun, the black car, the music chips, Tim's vacuum coffee maker, his clothes, everybody's clothes and toothbrushes—he wished he had brushed his teeth—and the pots and pan and the groceries would all be all right. That they could go back inside and forget it.

David pushed the buzzer. A woman's voice said, "Yes?"

"Hello," he said to the air. "My name is David Dai, I work for Mayla Ling, your neighbor? May we make a call from here?"

"Step back please?"

He assumed they were being surveyed.

"Ms. Magritte?" Mayla said.

"Oh, hello Ms. Ling." Then nothing. David looked at Mayla, wondered what was going on. Then he realized Ms. Magritte had to come down and let them in. So they waited and he ignored Mayla's house and the big steel doors.

Ms. Magritte's garage door opened. The domes on this street didn't have front doors. Or sidewalks or windows on the street or any of the other places and ways that neighbors were neighbors. "Hello, Ms. Ling," Ms. Magritte said, smiling. She was a tiny dark woman who spoke American-accented English. "Is there a problem with your system?"

"No," Mayla said, "there's a bomb in my house."

That struck Tim as funny.

Ms. Magritte did not know what to say.

"We have to call the police," Mayla said.

"Oh my God," Ms. Magritte said. She looked up and down the street as if she might see someone, and then at Mayla's garage doors. "Who—" Ms. Magritte started and then closed her mouth.

"I'm not political," Mayla said. "It's because of my position at the bank, I think."

Ms. Magritte nodded as if this explained something and led them upstairs. David relinquished Mayla to Tim's arm. He handed the cat to Mayla and was amused to realize that it was good there was no one else who needed watching because he was working against the law of diminishing returns. "Careful," he said, "he scratched me." Welts stood on his hand. Mayla nodded. Like Xhosa refugees, he thought. She would be all right as long as he could keep telling her what to do. Tim would be fine as long as he did not allow himself to realize. And he would be all right, he reflected wryly, as long as he had to keep telling her what to do.

"I have a Steuben glass bud vase from the 1900s," Mayla said to Ms. Magritte. "It was my grandmother's from Hawaii. I was afraid to take it to work because I was sure someone would knock it off my desk. Isn't that ironic? Of course, David says it may not go off. I guess I should have put it away where it would be safe but I always felt what's the use of having those kind of things if you don't leave them out where you can see them and enjoy them?"

Ms. Magritte licked her lips. "I think you should sit down and have a cup of coffee. Then after your man calls the police maybe I should call Girardin. Girardin is my husband, Ms. Ling, I'm sure you remember him?"

David made the call. He wanted to relate things crisply, not wasting words. Unfortunately the officer kept interrupting him, asking him about things before he'd gotten to them and then making him go back to explain. But he had been through this kind of thing before; people who did not know how to take a briefing. "No sir, I don't know when it got there . . . yes sir, a pressure trigger . . . yes sir, I've seen them before, in the war in South Africa . . . no sir, I'm not a citizen, I work for Ms. Ling . . . no sir, I've never seen one like it . . . the trigger, just the trigger, I've never seen liquid explosive . . . I don't know, it could be nitroglycerine for all I know, it looks transparent . . . nitroglycerine . . . no sir, I didn't say it was that. Nitroglycerine is something people used to use, like dynamite, a hundred years ago. It could be anything, I don't know . . . I was a chemist before the war . . . no sir, I don't know, I was just making the point that I do not recognize it, you see? I do not think it is nitroglycerine . . . no, I did not touch it, it would probably explode . . . yes sir, everybody is out . . . we will be waiting outside . . . yes sir, the watertight doors are shut. Goodbye—what? . . . David, David Dai . . . D, A, I . . . the records might be under Jean David Dai, that is my whole name . . . yes sir, that's right, Mayla Ling . . . yes, French . . . yes sir . . . thank you sir . . . good-bye.

David took back the cat and they thanked Ms. Magritte and went outside, standing together. They watched the door and looked up the street at the direction the police would come. The cat clung, curious and frightened. David's hand hurt where Meph had scratched him. He realized he was tapping nervously on his hip and made himself stop.

"This is crazy," Tim said to no one in particular. He kept shaking his head, as if this were some sort of amazing entertainment.

The sound of sirens set David's teeth on edge. It was a scream that bounced around stone tunnels and made it impossible to tell where the noise was coming from. It was unsafe under the artificial lights. Of course, lights were confusing for pilots in the old night-vision goggles the Prots used. Not like the new German goggles that compensated. He realized he was thinking they would use the lights to call in strikes. The first car rocked around the corner, a blue-and-white Julian patrol car. They turned the siren off but left the blue-and-white lights flashing and shifting across the walls and the street, glancing off the metal doors. Far off another screech was colliding with the walls and corners. Doors slammed, an officer pointed at them, he straightened up. He identified himself to the officer and said that he was the one who had called. The officer was black, one of ours, he thought. He told the young officer—whose eyes kept disappearing behind the polished visor of his cap when the light reflected off it—what he'd found and what they'd done (leaving out the part about the cat) and which doors they'd shut. While he was talking, a third and fourth car parked next to the first two, cutting off the back half of the street. He had to wait until they shut off their sirens to finish speaking. They left their lights on. It bothered his eyes. He wondered if he'd ever be able to stand the sun again.

The officer walked over to Mayla who was standing by the first car. He stopped, nodded respectfully. There were white officers and that seemed strange. In Africa he had worked with mostly black troops.

The cat squirmed. David relaxed and scratched his ears,

but Meph laid them back and mewed, his eyes slitted
against the flashing lights. A lower siren set Meph squall-
ing, a skid pulled up, lights flashing blue and green. Men in
combat beige overalls stepped out and began to pull out
equipment. Explosives Unit.

He shifted his shoulders and then realized he had no
rifle. An officer came up and told him to move back behind
the cars, out of the way. Of course, here it didn't matter
what color the officers were, this was not Afrique. People
had begun to collect and a civilian crew pulled up and took
out vid equipment. Mayla was talking to someone, her
hands were in motion as she explained something. From
where he stood her eyes were hidden by the shadow of her
hair except when the light from the cars swept across her
face. Then the blue light made her face perfectly white, and
her eyes, hair and mouth were as black as water.

"Lieutenant," someone said to his left and he turned but
it was an officer talking to one of the men from the skid.
Meph mewed and he realized he was squeezing too hard.
Relax, he told himself. He was waiting for the explosion
and he knew when it came he was going to start, he was
wound up tight and there was nothing he could do except
wait.

"Is this like the bomb on Esperance?"

"I think. Nobody's seen it yet. One of her staff described
it," the lieutenant said.

"They usually go off."

"Either they do when they come in or they don't at all,"
the lieutenant said. "Usually once they've fucked with the
trigger it either works or it doesn't."

"What about Desalines?"

"That one had been there awhile. Usually, though, they
go off or they do not."

The officer nodded, "This one probably won't—"

The explosion was a thud-thump, the watertight doors
into the garage held for maybe a tenth of a second and
then there was the hammer blow of the water hitting the

main doors. The water immediately muted the sound, giving it an odd, flat quality.

Then silence.

David raised his head. He was behind a car with the cat shielded by his body. The force of the water hitting the big garage doors had warped them, bowed them out, but they must have been built to do that. The lights slid down one wall, across the street, angled up another wall and across the warped doors, meeting and forming and splintering again, back down the walls. He was the only person who had ducked, everyone else stood staring. He tensed for the firing to begin, or for the mortars to start elephant walking down the street.

Somebody whistled appreciatively.

David got up. This was just his job, no one was going to start shooting. He looked at Mayla, standing next to an officer, staring at the doors, and she was not anyone he knew.

Screw it. Someone else was handling it. The walls rose up, more sharply than the spine of the ridge of highlands behind the wash, where Namibia and Kalahari almost met, about Rehoboth. His knee ached, remembering Rehoboth. He cradled the cat who was too frightened to complain. Nobody was looking at him. They were walking to the doors, or reaching into their cars to call the station.

An officer told the crowd to disperse. It was only a dozen people but David stepped back through them, became part of them, walked down the street trying to give the impression of purpose. He kept his head down and did not look back. At the end of the street he waited. The tunnel buses ran fairly often, although he'd never taken one, he'd seen them. He hoped he didn't have to wait long. He counted slowly, in French, and at 512 one coasted around the bend. He looked back.

Tim Bennet was tall enough and blond enough to stand out in the group. He was looking at David. Even from the distance David could tell.

He didn't know what to do. He expected Tim would shout, say something to someone. He put his foot on the step.

Tim Bennet was watching him, but he didn't move.

David got on and paid with change out of his pocket, "The cat is a problem?" he asked, hoping he would not have to get off and let the cat go, or walk.

"No problem," the driver said.

He hadn't even looked at the front of the bus to see if it said where it was going. He knew where he was going.

Away.

6

House Arrest

The blue and whites brought her home in a patrol car. She had to stand on the street and use the intercom to ask Jude to open the door. Then she had to go to her grandfather who was eating soup and tell him, "Someone blew up my house, sent a bomb in the mail and it blew up."

Her grandfather looked up at her, holding the spoon in his shaking hand. "What did you *do*?" he demanded.

He wasn't asking her what she did when it happened, he was asking her what she did to cause it.

"I don't know," she said, honestly. And then, to her great embarrassment, she felt the heat in her face and the threatening tears. She cleared her throat to explain that she thought that she was just in the wrong place at the wrong time, but when she tried to speak, her voice shook and broke. "I don't know," she managed again and he looked away.

He wanted her to stop crying. He didn't know what to do when she cried. He hated crying, it made him nervous.

He waited, and she looked at the vid. The vid was sitting on the counter where he could watch it while he ate. Jude had put on the mute when they came in, and a man and a woman were standing in a jungle, speaking intently and soundlessly to each other.

Finally she said again, "I don't know."

"You stay here, Mayla Lee," he said gently.

Just that. But it made her cry and Jude put his arms around her and told her it was all right, that she was safe now. Her grandfather stood up and patted her back awkwardly. She thought she was crying from gratitude. He was telling her that he loved her enough to bring her trouble into his house.

Anything could happen. And if anything could happen, then true love was trusting, wasn't it?

David Dai had disappeared. The blue and whites thought that it was possible that there had been collusion between David and Anna Eminike. An officer sat on the sheet-covered couch in Mayla's gram's sitting room. "It explains why he runs, and why he is hard to find. Because he has help to hide, you see?" The blue and white was a chubby young island boy with big eyes and an air of earnest helpfulness.

It didn't sound right to Mayla. If David were working with *La Mano de Diós* then why had he still been in the house when the bomb arrived?

"He was a dupe," the officer said. "*La Mano de Diós* used him. They didn't tell him the bomb was going to come."

"Why would he go to them for help to hide if they used him?"

"Maybe they had made a plan, not expecting him to be alive to use it. To make him think they would help him. And now he is using it."

She pointed out that David came to her immediately when he was approached in the parking.

The officer thought about this. "These people, anyone connected with *La Mano de Diós,* they all are under constant surveillance," he said. "Maybe they were afraid that we would find out that he was working with them. They met him in the parking, and to divert the suspicions of any watchers he pretended to turn them away." He nodded to himself, warming to his own theory, liking the taste of it in his mouth. "And when you were shot at in the parking the gunman had intended to miss. They were establishing Dai as a target."

"What was the point, the profit," she asked. "Why plant a spy in my house? There wasn't anything for them to learn, I don't have any information."

"Connections." He rolled his eyes. "*La Mano de Diós* looks for patterns."

God's surgeons. One event has innumerable ramifications, ripples in Mandelbrot patterns of chaos, and God told Anna Eminike the things to do to initiate God's patterns. Murder this person. Bomb that house. Sense in every moment, divine inspiration in every random action. God alone saw whole.

"We aren't saying that he is working with them," the officer said. "We're just considering the possibility." He made this qualification without real conviction. The sheet he was sitting on had a pattern of pale washed flowers in pink. Her gram had liked pink. Mayla's sheets were gone. She had not had any pink sheets in her whole house and now she was back sleeping on pink sheets.

"He'd only been here a month," Mayla said. "It's not very likely that they could recruit him and convert him in a month."

"Maybe he met Eminike in Africa," the officer said.

"That's pretty thin, isn't it?" she asked.

"Why did he run?" the officer asked.

She didn't know. That was the simple truth, she didn't know why he had run. She didn't know why her house was gone.

"I think he'd had it," Tim said. Tim had watched him get on the bus. He said David had just walked to the end of the street, waited until one came and got on.

"And you didn't think about stopping him?" The blue and white asked.

He just sounded curious but Tim squirmed. "I figured," Tim said, "if he wanted to tell somebody he would have. I wasn't thinking about him being a possible terrorist, I mean, he kept talking about how he wasn't the right person to work for Mayla and about going home and he said how he thought that this country was crazy. I just thought that enough had happened that the guy should be allowed to leave if he wanted to. I was beginning to wonder if it wouldn't be a good idea to go somewhere else, you know, standing out there."

"Where did you think he was going?" the officer asked.

"I don't know," Tim said.

"Did you think he would come back, get in touch? That he was going to see friends?"

"I wasn't thinking about anything," Tim said. "You know, Mayla's house had just been blown up." But then he shook his head. "No, I guess I wouldn't say he'd come back."

"Why not?" the officer said.

Tim stared at his hands. Finally he said, "If you'd seen him. Just the way he looked, you know."

"Try to explain," the officer said. He was smarter than he acted, more patient than Mayla has suspected and she suddenly felt a chill.

"I don't know, purposeful, I guess. Like . . . I don't know."

The officer prompted, "Purposeful. Like he knew where he was going?"

"Of course he knew where he was going," Tim said, "it's a bloody dead-end street. And no, I'm not saying he was going to meet some frigging terrorists."

"What are you saying?"

Tim shook his head. "If you'd seen him, you'd know what I mean."

"Ah," the blue and white said.

Oh God, Mayla thought, they were going to pin it on David.

Mayla's grandfather's house had breath—cool air moved in the rooms and the tall peacock feathers drifted—but no life. By Caribbean standards it was old. It had been built when the first and second levels of Julia were the only levels, sixty years ago. It was, in its way, a frontier house: built in a big square and starkly simple, just a concrete warren of blind rooms and corridors closed in on itself.

Her gram had tried to make it pretty. She had put mirrors on the walls to create windows and had filled the rooms with spindly wooden tables covered with lace and tall red and yellow Chinese vases filled with pale fronds of pampas grass and peacock feathers. When she was a girl Mayla had loved her gram's things.

The mirrors reflected mirrors on the opposite walls so that the tables covered with knickknacks and pictures of cousins and family and the Virgin in silver frames were reflected in infinite progression. Sometimes, from the corner of her eye, Mayla thought she saw movement in the rooms at the backs of the mirrors.

Paranoia. Or just plain fear.

She was back in her old room. The bed was still pink, the walls the palest rose. In the drawers were old things she hadn't bothered to take with her when she moved out: clothes ten years out of date, a bracelet with a little wirework horsecharm dangling off of it that was supposed to be a voudoun sign—they had been big when she was in school—and a box of hair solution to streak her hair metallic silver because Terez, who was her best friend, had streaked hers gold. She threw them out.

"What are you doing?" Jude asked her in the hall.

"Cleaning up my room," she said. Strange behavior, she

thought. Here she was, reduced to almost nothing but the clothes on her back, and she was throwing out whatever else she could find. She threw out everything in all the drawers. There were a couple of dresses in the closet that she could still wear to the bank. Her gray dress, the cliché of the banker gray dress, without style or taste but perfectly functional, she could wear that. Her oyster-colored dress. It had the funny Egyptian linen collar that made it look dated, but she would only wear it until she could get some more things.

In the top of the closet she found a shoe box with a rubber band around it. She slid it off the shelf thinking it was full of letters or something, but when she opened it up, it was full of picture cards. On top was a card of a conical volcano, perfect as a film set, not real.

She turned it over.

> Hi Princess,
> Things are beautiful in Bali! It's hot hot hot! I'm going to be here awhile, maybe in a few months I can bring you here for a visit.
>
> Love, Dad.

She looked at the date, she would have been eleven years old. When she was eleven her parents had been gone for five years. They had left when she was six.

When she was six. She closed her eyes and thought of being six. What was six? Her parents gone to see her grandfather's family in Hawaii. Cousins. Caribe had still been part of the U.S. First Hawaiian of Caribe was still connected to First Hawaiian of Honolulu and the Lings of Hawaii.

When she was six, Enzalo Estaves y Otoya launched a violent independence movement. She could see her gram filling the bathtubs with water in case it was shut off—although she pictured her gram as an old thin-legged lady in tights and a cardigan. When she was six her grandmother was, what, in her fifties? Her hair wasn't gray, she kept it blonde. With effort the blonde gram from ims could be superimposed. They grew algae in buckets and plastic tubs and they had an old-fashioned air recycler sitting in the kitchen, all in case the air was cut off. All of the house staff left except Jude, who cooked for them and ate with them. If the air went bad they planned to shut off most of the big house and live in the kitchen, bathroom and dining room, all four of them including Jude—but in their part of the city the air stayed good.

Her grandfather was home all of the time. President Enzalo Estaves y Otoya nationalized the bank. He sat around dressed like it was Sunday afternoon, in tights and shirts and alpargatas, sandals like slippers with cotton soles. He was angry all the time.

"Be quiet," her gram would say, "your grandfather is worried about a lot of things."

Her mother and father sent cards, first from Hawaii, then from Spain. The cards came in bunches wrapped in string, some of them sent three or four months before and some only two weeks old. Then nothing for a few months. The mail was "interrupted." Like someone speaking.

Her mother wrote that they had tried to call but couldn't get through, or that she had gotten a card or letter. When the calls did get through, her mother's voice was a foreign voice now, deep and rumbling, deeper than her father's voice had been at home. A stranger's voice like voices on the vid.

Her father sent picture cards with little notes on the back addressed to "Princess" or "Mayla Lee." The underwater mall complex financed by First Hawaiian U.S. at Waikiki. Mauna Loa. The Kamehameha Island Causeway. Then Moorish architecture of Grenada, a woman in a black lace mantilla, great expanses of golden field and narrow streets. Mayla kept the cards in her shoe box, rubberbanded together in packets the way they came. She sat on her bedroom floor and laid them out all around, some propped up against her pink bed, some on the floor, making up a vast, sun-drenched landscape. All the cards were full of such space, such light.

She stayed in her bedroom a lot. She remembered pieces of things. Her grandfather shouted at Gram that she was a weak, hysterical woman and Gram cried. She and Gram had packed cases with underwear and a change of clothes and Gram had sewn her engagement ring and her pavé cockatoo pin with the clock and the big ruby into the hem of Mayla's poncho. She connected her grandfather's shouting with the packing although she wasn't really sure they happened at the same time. She didn't remember ever actually leaving, where would they have gone? What was her Gram planning they should do, try to get to America? There were no subs running. Maybe her Gram meant to go to friends—but she couldn't think of who that might have been.

Her mind went back to playing on the floor of her bedroom, laying out cards, making landscapes of the woman in the lace mantilla dancing in front of Mauna Loa. The woman in the black lace mantilla was the only real person in any of the cards her father sent her. There were little people, far away—bent over in the fields, strolling through the streets of Grenada—but they were too small to be someone. The woman in the black lace mantilla had shiny black hair, and Mayla had black hair. The woman danced through the sunny bright places all by herself. She hoped her father would send her a postcard with a picture of another person, a friend for the Spanish lady.

She tried to remember more, but what came was later, when she was older. A memory of the yellow kitchen full of young men in black jackets, laughing and talking in Spanish. Waiters, sent by the caterer for big parties. She was older then, her grandfather was back at the bank. President Enzalo Estaves y Otoya had been arrested by Colonel Bustamante, who everyone called the Argentine. The Argentine became President-for-Life Bustamante. He declared the Revolution a failure, denationalized the bank, and her grandfather put on his suit and went back to work. Her grandfather became *una persona de influencia,* good friends with people from the government. Old men like De Silva and Chavez.

The parking was full of government cars again. That must have been when she went back to school. (She knew that Gram taught her at home, but what could the lessons have possibly been? Vague memories of workbooks.) She was enrolled in *La Escuela de las Órdenes de Los Desaparecidos,* a Catholic girl's school where despite the name, no Spanish was spoken. She got letters (from her mother) and picture cards (from her father) one at a time, not in bundles. From Tenerife, from Hawaii again, from Los Angeles, from Spain, and then the letters came from Madrid from her mother, and the picture cards came from her father in Barcelona. The letters finally started coming from Barcelona, but by then the picture cards were coming from Majorca, from Morocco, from Corsica, from Crete, then from Bermuda. The letters never moved from Barcelona, but the picture cards ranged farther and farther. And every time a letter came from Barcelona, her Gram frowned.

Her father called. She got to talk to him for a moment. She was accustomed to the way his voice sounded, so deep and foreign. Jimmy Ling was very tan, not very handsome. He didn't look Chinese like her grandfather, or American like her gram. He didn't really look like anyone she knew. "How are you, Mayla Lee?" he asked. "Are you studying? Did you get my card from Bermuda?"

She said she had.

"What did you think of that, pink beaches? They really are pink, isn't that amazing? Would you like to come and see a pink beach? Your Dad is going to make money, a big real estate deal, and then maybe you can come to Bermuda."

The picture card from Bermuda had shown green hills, a

big white building with tiny figures in red coats in front of it. No beach.

Her Gram said, "Jimmy, don't promise the child things you might not be able to do."

"Marceline is still in Barcelona," he said to Gram. "She's staying in Barcelona, I'm getting a divorce. I don't know why you get that look, mom, you always bitched about Marceline. I can't please you, I can't please dad. I'm damned if I do and damned if I don't."

"When are you coming home?" Gram asked tightly.

"I have a business," he said, his voice climbing although not high enough to sound like a Caribbean voice. "Things are busy right now. As soon as I get this thing wrapped up in Bermuda. You'll see, it's really going well, not like Majorca. I didn't know enough about the market in Majorca, and besides, that was all that European old-boy network. I'm working with some local people here, it's going very well, mom. Tell dad I'm doing very well, I'll call you."

The second picture card from Bermuda arrived two days later. The beach was pink, but so was the sky. Skies were supposed to be blue, which made the whole picture suspect anyway. She put it in the shoe box with the other picture cards.

The card on top of the Bermuda beach was dated four or five months later and came from Tenerife, a picture of yellow birds. She had never gone to Bermuda or Bali.

She sat on the pink bed in her grandfather's house and looked at the picture card from Bali. Had it been the last one? Or had he continued to send them for awhile and she just hadn't bothered to put them in the shoe box?

She put the rubber band back around the shoe box and put it back in the closet. She didn't throw anything else out.

7

Dedale

David sat down on the bed. Yesterday when he'd taken the room he'd declined to rent the vid, but today he'd gone back and paid for a week. 2cr a week, that brought his rent to 37cr a week. He didn't have any chips to play on it so he was forced to watch Caribbean broadcasts or American imports—sometimes dubbed in Spanish or Creole. He didn't like soap operas or news, but at least it was noise.

He and Meph were living in one room, with a tiny flash unit, a cooler about a meter high and a sink. The walls were painted bluish-green, the color made it feel colder. The walls were visible all the time because he couldn't sleep without the light on. The bed didn't heat properly either.

"In a couple of weeks, we'll go home," he told Meph. Meph, who was sitting by the door gazing off into space, mewed to be let out. "To a place where there is sun and we can get warm. It is summer there, you know?" He added hours, ticking on his fingers. "It is late in the morning, in a little bit it will be lunchtime."

It was 6:30 p.m. here, he'd have known even without the vid because his neighbor in number three was just home. He heard him come in and then he heard crowd noises and the voice of the sports announcer. He couldn't hear clearly through the walls but he could tell that the sports announcer was speaking Spanish. A soccer game. David flicked through the offerings. Nicaragua and San Salvador. On the other side the neighbor in number five did not get back until midnight. Not that time mattered in Caribe, there wasn't any daylight, day shift, night shift, it was all the same. When number five got in at midnight he apparently started dragging plastic chairs all over his room. At least that was what it sounded like.

The dehumidifier clicked on. It was noisy, but outside the air was more humid than it had been on the upper levels where Mayla lived and worked.

David watched Nicaragua beat San Salvador.

Sometimes the cat would come crawl in his lap. He clucked his tongue but Meph was ignoring him, crouched by the door, staring at the wall as if he could see through it and watch number three's soccer game. Abruptly Meph flicked his ears back, then looked at the back wall, listening. David listened, too. After a few seconds he heard the rumbling. A freight line ran in back of them, tuneled through rock. He didn't hear it so much as feel it, but he was getting accustomed to it.

This morning the Sunday paper had a little story about the bombing. Terrorists. Political elements. Linked with the bombing of the minister's dome. It said Ms. Ling's driver had left the scene and was currently sought for questioning. He did not think he should be any part of "wanted for questioning."

Hide. And wait. Eventually maybe it would get quiet and he could leave. Maybe a month, two months. He did not have a passport anymore. He had money. When he got on the bus the morning the bomb went off it had taken him to the central terminal and when he got off he saw the row of bank machines. He tried the bank machine there and his funds had not been frozen so he took out everything. It had taken almost ten minutes; the system had done a retinal scan and then asked him to wait and he had waited and waited, wondering if a blue and white was going to show up. But finally it had given him the money. At home the machines would not do that, they would only give a certain amount.

Then he had tried to decide where to go. The buses were all different. Good buses were clean and had company names on the side; *L'Exprimier* and *Garrara Transportation Company*. The worst buses were the *taptaps*. Psychedelically colored rattle traps. People waited patiently in line for the good buses and most got seats. When a taptap pulled in the disembarking passengers had to force their way though crowds of middle-aged women with shopping bags and young women with too much makeup and metallic colored hair. They forced their way on, shoving, while young men in jackets the shimmering blue and green of dragonflies waited leaning against the wall.

So he got on a taptap marked "Dedale" because he knew he couldn't hide in a neighborhood like Mayla's. What would he do, knock on garage doors until someone like Mrs. Magritte called the blue and whites? Besides, *dedale* meant "labyrinth" in French. It had seemed like a good place to hide.

And here he was.

He fixed dinner and he and Meph ate. Meph seemed to get a great deal more out of the tile fish than he did. Maybe if he had mustard he could hide some of the fish taste; it wasn't that he hated fish, he just got so tired of it. Then they watched the vid. Then he got up and did some exercises, calisthenics and isometrics using the door frame and stretching exercises. And then he flopped back on the bed, listless. Doing nothing all day was oddly tiring, but he didn't feel ready to sleep. Meph was curled up on the pillow. He watched more vid, a movie from Brazil dubbed in English about a man whose wife and lover poisoned him with fugu fish toxin, but the man only went into a coma and his friend the doctor realized and substituted the corpse of an indigent. Most of the movie was about the husband's revenge. He was supposed to sympathize with the husband but he found everybody in the movie unlikable.

Eventually the neighbor in number five got home and started dragging the plastic chairs around.

After that stopped, nothing to do but try to go to sleep.

The walls bounced the light back at him. They were bluish-green, low-rent lacquer glossy, chill. Maybe if he turned off the light it wouldn't seem so cold. It was ridiculous for a grown man to sleep with a light on. He settled Meph and turned off the light.

He lay on his back. The bed was underneath him, he could feel it firm and steady. There was no light except a faint line around the curtains in the window because the corridor lights were on all the time. Like the lights around Mayla's dome. It was so dark he couldn't see the white of the sheets. He concentrated on the bed. He would build the room in his mind, then he would not feel as if he were drifting. A frame, a mattress that would only get warm on the left side and in one patch in the upper right corner. The cat asleep under the blanket against his waist. On his right. Very important to be oriented. He wondered which direction he was lying in, he knew north from south when he was driving on the belt. The belt was a circle around the first level of the city, the only level of Julia aboveground, and Julia was mostly inscribed within it except for a couple of arms thrown out like the part that Mayla's house had been in. He tried to orient this street within that circle but he didn't know how it was. He should be able to remember the bus route, orient that way. In his head he could construct the route of the first bus he'd taken, from Mayla's house to the city. Then he'd cleaned out his account and taken another bus, a *1* Center St. to *6* Sphinx Rd., a bus from the first level to the sixth level. But he couldn't remember the whole trip, couldn't get all the turns. Lying in bed he didn't know if his head was pointed north or east, south or west. He could feel his heart pounding. Why should it matter that he didn't know if his head was pointed north or south or east or west? People went their whole lives not knowing which direction they were lying when they slept. (His heart was pounding anyway. Foolish heart, there was nothing to be afraid of here. He felt so disoriented.)

Forget it. The bed was parallel to the road. The road was to the right. He was lying in bed on his back. The cat was on his right side. Even though he couldn't see it, the vid was at his feet. His feet were pointing at twelve o'clock. The door was about two meters away at about two o'clock. The sink, etc., was at his left, at nine o'clock, the bureau with the blue metal lamp on it was at eleven o'clock. And the other blue metal lamp was on his right, on the bedside table.

At ten o'clock was the door to the bath. Hold it in his head, hold the room. Cup it there. Even if it was not visible it was looming, solid, surrounding him. Now he knew where he was, relative to the room. Relative position was the best anyone could ever do anyway. He had studied science, he knew that. Absolute position was a myth. Heisenberg. The Uncertainty Principle. What was his spin?

He took a deep breath to try and calm himself. It was the dark. Stupid for a grown man to be afraid of the dark. Orient himself. The ceiling above him was dark. Above that, the fifth level and the fourth, and so on, all the way up to the ocean. And then two hundred meters of saltwater, then warm air, and stars, and he imagined a big silver moon. Closing his eyes he found it easier to imagine that than the room. His bed floating on a warm ocean.

Ursa Minor, Ursa Major, Cassiopeia, Orion, Draco, the
Pleiades. . . .

Could they see Draco this far south? Ursa Minor? They
weren't far enough south for the Southern Cross, they
were north of the equator.

But once the Cross had entered his sky he couldn't get it
out. It hung there, brilliant, not quite symmetrical. Perhaps because in the time he'd spent south of the equator
he'd been outside at night, he'd considered the African
sky. Now that sky—or some sky he had imagined contain-
ing the Southern Cross—spread broad and vast above
him. He turned on his side. He was not under that sky, he
was in a room a couple of hundred meters under the ocean.
He touched Meph whose breath swelled his tiny belly. So
fragile. David clasped his hand over Meph's belly, imagin-
ing what he could do, how vulnerable Mephisto was. He
tried to feel those tiny ivory ribs. Tried to feel even fear in
that to bring him back to the room. But the sky was still
above him. He made himself feel the bed that was only
warm on the right. His heart was pounding, he was sweating. His body was doing all the things a body did when it
was terrified, but he didn't feel any fear. Oh God, he hated
this. His heart pounding. Maybe he was having a heart attack? No, he knew he was not having a heart attack, just
afraid. Afraid of the dark. Give in to the fear, let the fear
swallow him, maybe he would come out the other side?
The bed was perched on a *kopje* in the Transvaal, night-
colored bluegreen, under the Southern Cross. Around
him, miles of dry grass, the *bandu,* and twisted *enkeldoring,*
dry branches rubbing and whispering in the hot January
wind. He opened his eyes but it was so dark it was as if they
were closed. The stars were distant, white, cold. So far
away, so old. He was so small. He couldn't do anything
with the fear.

He sat up, Meph mewed, he fumbled until he found the
touchplate on the lamp. Light. A room with cold, bluish-
green walls. He pushed back the blankets, scooped Meph

up and held the sleepy and irritated kitten against his chest, crooning to him in French and English.

"You son of a bitch," he whispered to Meph, "you sweet fucking bastard, *Mephisto, ma petit merde.*"

By Monday morning he had to get out. Meph tried to get past him but he got the door shut. The curtains stirred and Meph was on the windowsill watching, mouth opened soundlessly, pink and demanding. It was not fair. If he felt cooped up, then Meph felt cooped up, too.

"Life is not fair," he told the kitten. Meph wailed again, eerily silent behind the glass, and then batted at a drop of condensation running on the outside of the window.

It was so damp, air he could smell and faintly taste. Musty, old socks air. The air wasn't as good as it was on the upper levels. The man who rented the rooms was walking the length of the pink concrete hall, spraying fungicide again. The smell was faintly sweet. "Good morning, Señor Park," the man said.

David nodded and smiled and walked the other way. He had registered as Kim Park. He had said he was Korean— Park was a Korean name—but the man probably didn't know a Korean from a Zulu.

He had to decide what to do.

The smartest thing to do was to do nothing, to lie low and wait. To be invisible. But he didn't have a passport and if he was going to get out of Caribe he'd have to come up with one. Somewhere he thought he could buy a passport—but then he suspected he didn't have enough money to buy a black market passport. He did have enough to pay for passage to the U.S. If he could get to the U.S. he could explain to his uncle in Blacksburg and maybe they could help him get home?

Maybe if he waited the Caribbean police would arrest Anna Eminike and he would be cleared.

Then again, maybe he would win the national lottery.

Best to lie low for a few days and count on the inefficiency of the blue and whites. They would lose interest. Although they would probably flag his name so if he tried to buy a ticket for a sub they would be alerted.

There was a street name painted on the wall at the corner. Bestinata. Nothing was level here, streets did not feed into one another but were all on different levels. The whole area was haphazard: a true, three-dimensional maze. At the corner he climbed five concrete steps to a broader gray corridor going left and right.

No reason to choose left or right, so he went left. Cracked concrete "street," children playing crouched between plastic trash bins. They had a flowered rag on a string to make a wall, making smaller spaces in the narrow corridor. Some of the lights didn't work and he walked through a dim place. The air smelled of garbage and old socks. A little girl looked around the rag to watch him walk by. Her hair was in tight braids against her head. Her eyes were solemn and she rested her tiny hands on her dirty knees, her elbows stuck out like wings. Her sweater had faded blue and gilt butterflies on it.

That street emptied onto Plaza Del Malabarista. He had to go down three steps to get to the Plaza, it was about the width of a regular city street, and ran about six blocks.

The air smelled even worse here: unwashed bodies and curry over the dirty sock odor. The Plaza was rimmed with shops and the streets were full of vendors with vegetables set out on tables, homemade clothes on blankets, stalls that sold Indian food. He couldn't shake the feeling that he wasn't getting enough oxygen. He looked in shop windows; a pharmacy advertised antibiotics in bright foil envelopes, chrome and red and blue. Textiles piled like a still life, bright gaudy fabric patterned in gilt butterflies for saris and lamé for dance dresses.

Two girls and a boy were leaping into a square of walkway and leaping off, giggling. The littlest girl looked about five, she leaped and looked up at something invisible to David, shrieked and covered her mouth and jumped away.

Some advertisement activated when they came within range. The boy said something to the littlest girl and she hesitated, tortured by her desire to test again. She was at the stage when children are all legs. She leaped again—an exaggerated jump where she kicked up her red plastic shoes—and stood for a moment, watching. The oldest girl looked at David coming towards them. For a moment he wondered if he should cut through the vendors in the square, but the older girl called, "Aloka!" and they all ran.

He almost walked around the square where they had been playing; he didn't like VR advertisements. At home it was illegal to have them on a sidewalk or street. Here he figured that the lasers that tracked the viewer's eyes to feed the visuals weren't calibrated or maintained very often. He knew they were low power and that people didn't really get blinded in freak accidents. . . .

What had the children found so fascinating? He stepped onto the sidewalk and looked up at the shop.

Marquesa Mariposa. Was it a beauty parlor? A teenaged girl appeared on the sidewalk—or rather, not quite on the sidewalk, the image wasn't angled precisely and her feet were a little above the ground. She crooned something to him in Spanish although she was wearing a robe more like a kimono, gauzy blue with veins of gold and silver in some sort of pattern. She opened the robe, and it spread like wings, butterfly wings, ah yes, *mariposa* meant butterfly—

She was nearly naked under the wings, just a gold g-string and a kind of silver bikini top that was more like two strands of fabric in an "x" across her chest barely wide enough to cover her nipples.

It was a VR peep parlor. *Mariposas,* "pretty girls." He almost jumped in his hurry to get off the square and looked around to see if anyone had seen him standing there like some old man looking for a thrill. He couldn't tell if anyone had been looking at him. His face burned.

Go back to the room, he thought.

But he couldn't face that, either.

Stairs cut up to his left between two shops so he headed
up them, a long narrow flight of concrete stairs that left
him breathless. Another street of residences. He was afraid
he'd get lost, but if he just headed straight he figured he
could always turn around and get back to the Plaza. The
streets weren't ever very long here, anyway.

This street felt different, the flats were mostly whitewashed instead of blue or yellow and the people were Creole rather than Indian. He felt foreign. Women leaned on
windowsills chattering in Creole, but they stopped talking
when he passed and stared. Children stared at him, too.

This street emptied out on another shopping plaza,
smaller than the first. Painted high on the wall it said *Parish Jeramie.* Nothing here he hadn't already seen except
that the street vendor sold coconut bread and stew. Maybe
he would walk around once and then he would go back to
the Plaza and buy some tortillas and beans for lunch.
Maybe some rice. And catfood.

The storefronts were whitewashed or pale blue, some
with rainbows and snakes around the doors. The paint
peeled from the damp concrete. He wished he were home.
The homesickness came overwhelming and sharp and his
eyes watered with the intensity of it. He wanted to go to
the port, buy a ticket and get on the sub, be home in a day,
have his life back.

Foolish thing to do, but he wanted to so badly. Maybe
he could just go to the port and see what tickets cost. He
could apply to the French Consulate and get his passport
replaced, maybe the police would not notice, they were so
sloppy here—

All it would take was one flag in the system.

Plazoleta D'Imagen. Reality Parlor. Naive illustrations
leaped around the door, green men carrying blazing guns,
little more than stick figures, women with exaggerated
breasts swooning in lovers' arms. He was not interested, he
would go home and watch the vid.

He turned around to head back to the stairs and saw the

blue and whites, three of them, coming through the crowd. Just walking, purposeful. Without a thought he stepped into the reality parlor, pushing aside the black curtain. The girl behind the counter looked up.

"How much for a booth?" he said, because she was looking at him. Because he had come in here.

She stared at him, too. "One hour? Three hours?" she asked.

"An hour."

"Six cerciorcados," she said holding up the requisite number of fingers as if he might not understand her.

He gave her the money and she pulled a cardboard box out from under the counter and found him a pair of gloves that fit. She gave him a cotton haircover, too. The exit was at his back, he was listening for the blue and whites to pass, but the street sounds were muted by the curtain. He didn't think the blue and whites had been looking for him since they had not acted like they saw him or cared. He should have just walked past them. He pushed through a second curtain—almost running into a tall, long-armed boy who looked about sixteen.

The booth was small, three walls made of plastic partitions and the fourth the concrete back wall of the building. There was a worn, black plastic visor, the padding and the forehead was split and stuffing bulged out. And there was a treadmill and a set of handlebars hung from the ceiling.

What was he doing here? He sat down on the edge of the treadmill. Maybe he would just sit here for a few moments. He was just nervous, that was all. He would go back to the room.

He could try the games here, see what was on the network.

The visor was too big and felt heavy, he wondered how many people had worn it? He was glad for the cotton haircover. He stepped onto the treadmill and grabbed the handlebars suspended from the ceiling. He pulled the visor down.

Then he saw a room. Most of the room was a sketch-work of line, not a real room. He could see his schematic hands glowing like phosphorescent bones. Hanging in the middle of the room were the glowing words CREOLE, ENGLISH, SPANISH.

He raised his glowing hand and pointed to English with a bony finger.

"Welcome to the Parish Jeramie Reality Parlor. Please give your system name." The voice was female, cool and husky, American.

His system name when he was a kid had always been Lezard because that was the name of a character from the vid. "Lezard," he said.

"That configuration is new to this system. Do you have another name for this system?"

"No," he said.

"Please enter your personal information on the index." A schematic keyboard appeared in front of him and a form. Name: he typed "Kim Park." The gloves had feedback so he could feel resistance when he typed, as if he was hitting keys. Age: "34," Sex: "Male."

Address: He skipped that. Body Configuration: At the top of the form it said he could ask for a catalogue so he did.

The room suddenly fleshed out and the cool, female voice said, "A catalogue requires full system, this time will be counted as part of your hour."

He didn't care, he was just killing time.

The catalogue was the size of a magazine, and the gloves were too clumsy to turn the pages so he had to press the icons at the top. There was an icon for male—circle and arrow, an icon for female—circle and cross, an icon of a doctor's caduceus, an icon that said ZOO, an icon of a gear, and an icon of an arrow pointing to the right to page through. He pressed the icon for males.

And laughed at the first body. Big, black, broad-shoul-dered, immensely handsome body-builder type. Not interested. He paged through the stock bodies pretty quickly; a couple of vid stars and some model-looking types, a Haitian street boy, a Latino street boy, a white street boy, an Indian street boy, a Native American street boy, an oriental street boy. A soldier in camouflage, sports figures, a wizard in robes, a knight in chainmail, cliché after cliché. Then exaggerated types, metal bodies: chrome, silver, bronze, aluminum white, matte black, metallic red, blue, green. Leather bodies, neon bodies, negatives.

He ran completely through the males without finding any image he could imagine assuming and found himself in the female section looking at Denise Deren, the American VR star, who he admitted was very pretty with her green eyes and pale hair but who he also could not imagine wearing, so he pressed the caduceus.

A doctor looked at him out of an American-style surgical p-suit. "Normal human or other?" the doctor asked.

He didn't want to be chrome so he typed "yes" and for gender he typed male. Gave a height of 1.8 meters—hell, he might as well be tall. A weight, and a schematic of a generic male body appeared. He increased the weight by five kilos, decided that made the body look a little like the body builder on the first page and took it off. He was presented with a range of skin colors. He thought a moment, chose something dark. It would be nice to blend in. That meant curly black hair, close to the head. A presentation of eyes and noses and mouths and he chose pretty quickly. Then clothes and he just picked a sweater and tights. Normal, just look normal.

"Save this body as Lezard?"

"Okay," he said. And he had a body. The gloves were gone.

"Continue browsing?"

He started to say no then thought of the zoo. That would be interesting.

The first page was a dragon, sea green with red eyes and huge wings. He laughed again. No, he did not want to be a dragon. Not a demon with a face like leather and bat-wings. Not a winged horse, either. A whale, a green-tailed mermaid, an angel (luminous and quite pretty in an androgynous way but certainly not him.) A tall elf with long silver hair and green eyes and pointed ears. Alien creatures, part human, part leopard, or lizard or horse. A snake with beautiful scales like bright green and copper glass. Funny figures, fat old men and Charlie Chaplin and cartoon people. Then traditional animals.

An animal, that was appealing. He would like to be an animal. Not a lizard, despite his choice of names. He paged through thoughtfully. An owl, a hawk, a bat, a gazelle, a lion, a horse, a number of kinds of dogs, a wolf, a cat. . . .

A cat. He had never really thought of himself as catlike, but maybe a cat. But then he would have no hands. Maybe not.

The next section was all machines: planes and tanks and cars. He did not want to be a car, either.

He sighed and closed the catalogue.

Now there was a door in the wall. He grabbed the handlebars and took a step, the treadmill activated with a slight lurch and he was walking towards the door. The door opened.

It had been a long time since he did anything like this, maybe since the militaire. He had done simulations in training, there, but most of those had either been at consoles or in body suits. It was a little strange remembering that if he turned the handlebars he *turned,* even though his feet kept going straight on the treadmill.

The door opened on a playground. It didn't look real, wasn't supposed to. Everything in it was geometric, smooth, perfect in silver and red, surrounded by water and plashing with fountains. The pillars reflected his image in curving chrome. It all looked dated, like something that had been popular when he was a kid.

It was crowded but places like this were always a little crowded. If there weren't enough people the system generated a crowd. He looked up and the top of the fountains were crowned with blue gas flames. He sighed.

Actually getting here was a lot less interesting than picking a persona. In picking a persona there was so much potential. Like getting dressed for a party.

He looked until he found the access portals in the pillars in the center of the playground. (They had huge red metal balls bouncing up and down on top of them.) He could probably leave now, he had only ducked in because of the police, who were not even looking for him. Paranoia. He could go back to the apartment and Meph.

And do what?

"Time available?" he asked.

42.27, 42.26, 42.25, 42.24, 42.23. The time left blinked in front of him for five seconds and then disappeared.

Might as well play a game or something. He started forward and the treadmill started under his feet. Strange sense of being two places at once, in the playground *and* in the cubicle wearing the visor and gloves.

The systems available were listed at the access portals and there were people standing there reading. He had to kind of peer around. Some of the titles were dark, he supposed those were either not up and running or required membership. Flight simulations, adventure games with wizards, romances, combat games, after the eco disaster games, mysteries, a pirate simulation/adventure that had been popular when he was a kid. . . .

"We need a sixth," said a beautiful Latino woman with an eyepatch. The fact that she was beautiful didn't mean anything, anybody could be beautiful. "Is there anyone here interested in making a sixth?"

"Everything here is chaff," said a tall blond American male with a distinct Caribbean accent.

"It all looks system generated," the woman said.

It was easy to pick out the five users, once he knew there

were five; besides the one-eyed woman and the American blond there was a tall, saturnine-looking fellow with an earring and an alligator tattoo on his arm, a woman with silk-white hair like fine egret feathers, and a fey-looking young man with copper hair and green eyes who probably spent too much time playing wizard adventure games. The copper-haired young man was looking at him. "He's not phantom," Copper Hair said.

"Sure he is," the one-eyed woman said.

"No he's not," Copper Hair said. "You're not, are you? You want to play?"

David shrugged. "I do not know the games, and I only have forty more minutes left."

"How the fuck you do that, Monode!" Alligator Tattoo said.

"He don't act like a phantom," Copper Hair said. "Phantoms don't stand still when you look at them, they have to do something."

"I'll pay for some extra time," One-Eyed Woman said.

"I got change, too," Alligator Tattoo said.

"It is not a problem," David said, "I can pay. What do I say to get out?"

"System," said Alligator Tattoo and flickered out of existence. In a second he was back. " 'Recommencer' will bring you right back to here."

"System," David said, and the world went black. He lifted the visor and went back out to the counter and bought two more hours. The five were still waiting when he came back.

They were in a virtual adventure league and they were playing a war-game simulation called *Zone of Fire*. Somebody hadn't shown up and if they hadn't found a sixth they'd have had to forfeit. "You don't have to do nothing, I mean, unless you want to," said Alligator Tattoo. Alligator Tattoo was clearly much younger than his persona. They all called him Chaco, except for the copper-haired boy, who called him Santos.

The portal opened and they stepped into an arid landscape, a field of dry grass. Almost, but not quite, the landscape of the Transvaal. The light was bright and hard and under it he felt himself expand. "Where are we?" he asked.

"Argentina," the one-eyed woman said.

Behind them were hills, in front of them was the long flat expanse of wheat he supposed was the pampas. The wind bent down the grass but he couldn't feel it. The light! The light was so wonderful. He blinked, his eyes watering. Driving out the darkness, the dimness of Caribe. He could sleep in a light such as this, he could live in a light such as this.

"Base camp is there," the blond said. In the strong sunlight David could see that the blond was cyborged with a delicate tracery of chip at the temples, like a vid character in bad American science fiction. What was it supposed to do, make him faster? Make him see in the dark?

He thought of the look he had chosen and smiled to himself, he really did look plain.

The base camp was not what he had expected. There was a tent, a tank, a collapsed glider and enormous amounts of ordinance. No mess, nothing for living. It wasn't at all real. People knew what they were doing; the blond American clambered into the tank—he must have been sitting at a console rather than using a treadmill—and Alligator Tattoo started handing out rifles. The rifles looked familiar enough, AP30s, cousins to the rifle he had carried in Anzania. When he took the rifle the glove tried to simulate weight by locking up and contracting. It didn't really feel as if the rifle weighed anything. David wondered how he was supposed to shoot and keep one hand on the handlebars. He tried to shoot the bolt, but the action wasn't smooth.

Alligator Tattoo—what was his name? Santos?—said, "What are you doing?"

"Checking the," how did you say it? "ah, the barrel."

He shrugged. "Just trying to do something." He turned it over and looked at the clip. "How much ammunition?"

"I don't know," Santos said. "You don't have to reload."

"Ah," David said, "that is convenient."

"You ever shoot one before?"

"An AP30, only a couple of times. I have shot an AP15."

"Yeah?" Strange but the look, the tattoos, the body language and voice and expressions all fit a man older than David but Santos sounded young, maybe eighteen or nineteen. "Were you in Brasil?"

"No," David said.

Santos didn't know what to say. The one-eyed woman was looking at them, and the copper haired boy.

"I was in Anzania," David said into the silence. He didn't know if they would believe him or not, he couldn't remember any Central or South American troops in Anzania. This was a mistake. He should not have done this. He was aware of standing on the treadmill, his knee was starting to ache a little.

On the other hand, these people didn't know who he was. There was no way they could ever find out what he looked liked. He was free to relax, to tell them the truth as long as he didn't tell them his real name. "I am Lezard," he said. "You are Santos?"

Alligator Tattoo frowned, "Santos or Chaco. My call name here is Chaco. That's Monode—"

"Cobre," the boy corrected.

"Si, Cobre or Monode, whichever. The chico who drives the tank is Jack Stomper, the sarge is Amazon Lil," the woman with the eyepatch, "and that is Gin." Gin shook back her egret hair and smiled.

There was a crunch and the landscape around them shook, although the feeling was not translated into sensation. "Ay, cabrón!" the blond said and yanked the hatch down. The one-eyed woman clicked on a communications port and called coordinates. The tank pivoted, treads reversing and churning up grass—that was a nice touch, David thought—and moving out.

"Lezard!" Santos shouted, "come with me! Touch that Kessler!"

David obediently touched the big Kessler gun and it rumbled to life.

"Follow me!" Santos said.

Santos' Kessler was following him like a big dog. As David followed, "his" Kessler trundled docilely behind him. He couldn't help it, he started to laugh.

Santos glanced over his shoulder and grinned. "Do like this," he tapped his headset—where had he gotten a headset? David reached up and lo and behold, he was wearing a headset. When he tapped it suddenly he heard Amazon Lil talking in his ear, "Santos, you and Lezard head up around 14.5 and see if you can get a little mortar action on that ridge." Talking like a movie, he thought. Around him he could see red digital readouts, like looking through a heads-up display.

This was nothing like a real battle, he thought. Thank goodness.

David called his Kessler "Fido." Fido was behind him while he and Santos planned what kind of fire to lay down. They were "lying" behind cover. It didn't feel as if they were lying because he was still standing on the treadmill and his knee was aching enough that he couldn't forget it was there. Still, he was having a very good time.

"They are there, I think," he told Santos. He didn't really know, but Amazon Lil thought that a team like him and Santos would be there. He picked over the land. He could make decisions about where they might be if this were real, but the restraints on the system made different things work.

"We'll lay down fire," Santos said.

"Okay, you want we should elephant walk the shells?"

"¿Qué?" Santos said.

"It is a pattern, better than just a grid, because it forces your enemy to fall back behind the fire. You lay a diagonal line of fire, and then another line behind it, and then another line behind it. See, they will go back, away from the line up towards 13.4, 13.3," he pointed to the coordinates. "Then after they learn our pattern, say five, six rounds, we fire on their position, where we think they have run, where we gave them to run. Then if we have enough shells, we can do again."

Santos nodded. "Okay. Okay. This, this is what they do in real war, right?"

"Yes," David said. Of course, in a real battle he would probably prefer to set the gun emplacement and fall back, so when the firing started they would not be targeted. But that wouldn't work if Fido was going to follow him around. Santos told him that if they got up, the Kesslers would stop firing and follow them.

Santos showed him how to set the guns and key in the pattern.

"Once we shoot, they will shoot back at us, no?" David said.

"Si, they'll have our position."

It was only a game. It didn't matter. Still, it made him uncomfortable, knowing he was going to be exposed. Maybe they would get lucky, take out the other team's guns. "Okay, Fido," he said, "it's time."

The sound from the Kesslers was startlingly loud. The sound deafened him and he closed his eyes, feeling the handlebars, the treadmill, the visor resting on his forehead. "Fuck," he said to nothing in particular.

The krump krump krump krump of the mortars across the grassland was pretty realistic, too, he thought. But now the others had their range. His only hope was that they were too busy running to stop and fire. Krump krump krump krump. Krump krump krump krump. Elephant

HALF THE DAY IS NIGHT

walking. He'd seen the fucking elephant, like the Australians said when someone got wounded or killed.

It *was* nice not to have to worry about ammunition.

Krump krump krump krump. And then the pattern changed to angle the other way, to catch a team in retreat. Krump krump krump KRA-THUM-krump.

"We got a Kessler!" Santos shouted. "Come on! Vamos!"

"One more walk," David said. Krump KRA-THUM-krump, the sound of the exploding gun swallowing the motor sounds.

"Two of them! Slap, man! Now we split so they can only get one of us! Down the hill and watch for the glider!"

Down the hill. It didn't feel like down the hill, the tread-mill didn't tilt, the ground wasn't uneven. David just walked, pushing the handlebars to indicate speed, but he and the Kessler zoomed downhill, it bobbing and swaying as if traveling fast over uneven ground. In his headset he heard Santos reporting, "Two Kesslers, Sarge!"

"Clear," Amazon Lil said. "Fallback Al."

Fallback Al? What did that mean?

"Ah, fuck!" Santos said. "Lezard! I didn't tell you the fallback patterns!"

"Ears on the line! Com clear!" Amazon Lil said sharply. Vid army talk that said the channel wasn't secure and the enemy was listening.

"I just keep my nose clean then," David said.

All he needed to do was hide. Although that was hard to do with the Kessler rumbling along behind him. He tried to keep close to the ridge, on the flat grassland the Kessler would stand out like an oil derrick. Camouflage nets would help, heat reflecting nets. Break up the signature of the Kessler. He should ask Santos if they could get any.

The grass swished around him, he wished he could feel the wind. Still, the sunlight was so nice. And he was sweating from excitement. He was, he had to admit, having a hell of a time.

Were there mines?

Nothing to do if there were, he couldn't get the Kessler to go in front of him. He should have asked more about the rules. Next time.

Too late he caught a glimpse of something and looked up. "Watch for the glider," Santos had said. Although what he was supposed to do when he saw it—

"Glider above me at 15.4," he said, just as a woman with a banner of black hair leaned over the side and dropped something. He tried to push the handlebars out to go faster and there was this tremendous noise, the world went red, then black—

And he was in the playground. His ears were ringing. Around him stood phantoms, talking and laughing. He caught his reflection, a tall black man in a green sweater looking back out of the curving chrome of the pillar. He laughed a shaky laugh.

The playground was darker than the simulation, like being inside rather than like being in strong sunlight. Like being in Caribe.

Of course. When you died you went to Caribe.

The day was half gone, time eaten up by the game. That was something, it was even fun. He stood on the treadmill, absently rubbing his knee, wondering what he should do next.

He should leave a message for somebody. He put the visor back on and went back to the playground. If one of them got killed while he was leaving the message then he'd run into them. He didn't want to do that. He didn't know why, but it just seemed easier to just leave a message and get off the system, not say anything about getting killed in the game.

He told the system he wanted to leave a message for Santos.

The system didn't recognize the name.

Shit. What was the other name they had called him? Something like chico. Chaco. Leave a message for Chaco?

The system pulled up a phantom of Chaco and it was Santos, alligator tattoo and all.

"Okay," David said. "Thanks, ah, tell everyone thanks. It was very interesting. Ah, and I have a good time. Sorry I get killed and all, I hope you win. Fin."

David pulled the visor and was back on the treadmill. Stupid message. He could never leave very good messages. And he knew his English had been bad. He thought about going back and changing it, but every moment he was in the playground increased the likelihood that one of the others would pop out.

Enough. It had been a nice time.

Now all he had to do was remember how to get back to his room. And maybe pick up something to eat. He was kind of hungry.

David didn't plan to go back, it just used some of his money and he should be saving. He didn't know what he was saving for, he was pretty sure he didn't have enough for a passport and every day he was here he spent a little on the room, and on food for him and Meph. Bleeding to death a drop at a time.

"I should get a job," he told Meph. A job would be nice, pass the time, bring a little money in instead of the money all going out. But he would have to have identification.

Maybe he should sell something? Make something? What could he possibly sell or make? If he didn't do something, sitting in this room was going to drive him crazy.

Meph was sitting on the windowsill, ignoring him. Meph wanted to go out. Every time he opened the door he was afraid Meph would get out, if the kitten got away he thought he would never see him again.

When he stood up Meph mewed, hopeful. "No," he said. "I am just going for a walk. You stay here."

Sure, just going for a walk. Well, he would just see if

Santos had left an answer to his message, see if they had won.

He didn't have to go back to the *Plazoleta D'Imagen,* but he didn't know of any others, so he went that way. The square was full of peddlers, but there were no children playing in front of the peep show, so the butterfly girl had no audience to activate her. He was careful not to walk near.

People still stared at him. How was he supposed to hide? Maybe he could get surgery? Change his face? He didn't even know who to ask to find a doctor who would do it. And he didn't want to change his face. He wanted to god-damn well go home.

Maybe if he cut his hair he would look more like these people. Not many people wore their hair down to their shoulders anymore. He would do that, see if it helped.

He shoulders ached from tension by the time he got to the Reality Parlor. At least it was the same girl. He paid for an hour. Just an hour. If he met anyone he could always pay for more.

There was a message for Lezard, the system told him as soon as he hooked in.

Santos, of course. David felt himself smiling, Santos' way of talking was so boyish, so completely at odds with the sinister-looking revolutionary persona he wore. "Hey, Lezard, you should have waited around! We won, five to four. You were the only person to get killed, but that was my fault because I didn't tell you where it is we fallback. And I did not tell you how to hide the Kessler. The thing you did, elephant walking the mortars, that was great!

"Anyway," Santos went on, "We play again on Satur-day. Zanaza is supposed to be here on Saturday, so we have the six, but maybe you can show up and if someone else can't come then you can play, you know?"

No, he really shouldn't. He couldn't. It was a waste of money, playing games when he should be planning what to do, figuring out a way out of this country.

But where was he going to start finding a way unless he talked to people? Through the system he could talk to people and they would never be able to tell anyone who he was, never be able to betray him to the blue and whites.

So he might, after all.

But maybe he should look more like the others? In a way, he was more obvious than if he were somehow, how could he describe it? Flashy.

He asked for the catalogue again, called up the doctor. What could he do, strange-colored eyes? He tried blue eyes. No. Green eyes. Eh. Not so much difference unless he made them really green, and that felt foolish. Red, orange, yellow, purple, metallic, stone and other. He couldn't even imagine trying purple eyes, metallic gave him the obvious choices (with or without pupil). Featureless bronze eyes seemed very distracting and rude and when he looked at his own image they made him uncomfortable. He looked, he thought, dead. Other was very strange. Pupils shaped like hourglasses, hearts, circles like snakes, shattered eyes, tiger eyes, goat eyes, lizard eyes (which was kind of funny), eyes that were hollow as if there was nothing in there except darkness, and to take that further, empty eyes that were like windows on galaxies.

He wiped that as quickly as he could.

One of the options for yellow eyes was a dark amber, almost like brown eyes but not quite. He liked that. It was a little different, but not something anybody would notice unless they looked close.

Then he changed clothes. Something a little stranger, maybe like a commando would wear? Sweater with a shoulder patch to rest a rifle butt, boots.

It looked a little foolish. He almost switched back. No, save now, he thought, before you change your mind.

He saved and then wandered into the playground. He stood at the list of games trying to decide what to play. He could go to Tokyo, go diving, be a spy, be lost on a spaceship . . . but nothing would take him to Paris. It would have been nice, even if it was a synthetic Paris.

Eventually he tried being a spy for awhile. There was an international module but if it took him to Paris he couldn't get that far. He stopped playing before his hour was up.

On the way back to the room he stopped and got his hair cut short. But he still felt foreign.

8

Mindgames

Mayla and Tim settled in to her grandfather's house and her grandfather had Jude open up the rooms and take the dust covers off the furniture. It raised dust and in the dry, carefully maintained air of her grandfather's house the dust hung, fine as fog. Mayla couldn't see it but she could feel it, cottony tasting, coating her tongue and the inside of her mouth. It dulled the mirrors, dulled the fabric of the furniture, dulled her sense of taste and smell and made her feel tired and thick. She ran her finger across the mirror and left a line. The service came in and cleaned and the mirrors looked as clear as windows, but the next day the dust was back.

Two men from the insurance people came out and sat on the pink flowered couch where she had sat while the blue and white asked Tim why David wasn't coming back. The older, shorter man had a gray unhealthy face. Mayla supposed he had good insurance, though.

"Will you be staying?" he asked.

"No," she said, "well, yes, for awhile." She wasn't going to rush into buying a place and it would take awhile for the insurance money to come through.

"You will move to the United States?" the gray-faced man asked.

"Pardon me?" she said.

"If you are not staying."

"Oh, no. No. I thought you meant would I be staying here, with my grandfather. I'm not leaving Caribe."

"Ah," he said. "You see, a lot of people do, after something like this."

Leave home.

He told her she needed to hire some security.

"I will," she said. "I plan to. As soon as things get settled, right now I don't have a place of my own."

"You need someone now," the gray-faced little man said.

"It's not like I don't have someone, Tim is still here," she pointed out.

Tim sat, listening, his empty hands loose on his knees.

"It has upset everything," she explained. "I have to tackle things, one at a time. There are some things at work that I have to take care of, and then I have to find a place to live. And since Tim is here, I have security."

"Ms. Ling," said the gray-faced little man, "if you are going to stay, we believe you need to hire someone professional."

"Okay," she said. She could understand why they didn't exactly consider Tim a professional. "As soon as I can." First, she had to settle the MaTE deal. If she settled the MaTE deal, everything would fall into place; she could think about things, she wouldn't have to worry about being a banker, about work. "It might take me a few weeks, right now I don't have any place where someone could live, do you understand?"

They did not understand, or rather, as they made clear,

she did not understand. Her insurance rates were going to triple, no matter who or what she hired.

"Triple?" she said.

The house had been bombed seven days ago. And if she did not hire someone within the next fourteen days, her insurance would be canceled. She was now in a "high risk group."

"Because you have been targeted, Ms. Ling." The little gray-faced man seemed sympathetic. "And your security is compromised." He said "promised," as if she had been promised something. "Because your staff is involved."

"David wasn't involved," she said, from habit more than conviction.

"Yes," the man said, "but he ran away. So, we insurers, we are conservative people, we have to assume the worst. I have a list of agencies," he checked his briefcase, but it was his partner who handed it to her, "ah, yes, there it is. They can send you people to interview. These agencies, they are approved, you see?"

"Yes," she said. She held the list and read the names and when she was done she couldn't remember what she'd read.

Tim sat with his hands on his knees and the two insurance men sat on the dusty flowered couch, all of them looking expectant, looking at her.

"Thank you," she said. And then, much to everyone's surprise, including her own, tears welled up in her eyes. She blinked and blinked, but she couldn't stop them.

"I need to go back to work, to establish a routine, but I'm unfocused," she explained to Tim. They were almost in Marincite. She was working again. Or she would be, just as soon as she got to Marincite and started. "I can't seem to put my attention on the things it's supposed to be on." The house had been gone for nine days and she had twelve more to find security. "I suppose it's normal, but I'm worried about the Marincite deal. I am not very focused, you know. I can make mistakes, say the wrong thing, because I'm not sharp. People don't make loans with stupid bankers." When she got back to Julia, she was going to make an appointment with a counselor.

"Somebody else could go," Tim said.

"No," she said. "There's this Saad Shamsi business, I have to die about that."

"What?" Tim said.

"It's *en la sombra,*" she said.

"No, what you said, you'd have to 'die about that'."

"Decide," she said. "I said 'decide about that'."

"No you didn't," Tim said, "you said 'die'."

"I meant 'decide'." She shook her head. "Don't go analyzing, Tim. That business about Freudian slips isn't true. It's medieval psychology."

"I didn't say anything about Freudian slips," he growled.

The sub lurched, lousy docking. At the subport in Miami, she thought, the docking system was automated and it was always smooth. Everything in Caribe was inept. Would she have been able to make it as a banker if she had had to in the U.S.? Or was she inept, too?

She didn't want to come back to Marincite, but she had to. She would stay for two days, then go back to Julia and hire some security and start thinking about a place to live. Routine. Establish a routine. Then she'd be fine. She was a competent person, she was just unsettled.

The first class waiting room was quiet. A dark-haired man in a business suit was standing at the gate, waiting, and she thought, that person looks like Saad Shamsi. She was worried about that, seeing Saad Shamsi everywhere like a guilty conscience.

It was Saad Shamsi. Her luck, just to happen to come in at the same time as Saad was supposed to be meeting someone.

Then he saw them and waved. He bent his head to talk to the woman at the gate, then handed her his smart card.

She passed it through a reader and he came through walking towards her with purpose.

"*Madre de Cristo,* I'm not ready for this," Mayla said to Tim.

Tim frowned.

She smiled at Saad as if she was happy to see him.

"Mayla," he said. "Mr. Navarro thought maybe it would be better if someone you knew met you." He held out his hand and she shook it.

What did that mean? Was Polly Navarro telling her that she should give Saad his loan? Or was he thinking that after losing her house she would feel better recognizing her escort?

Saad was with the city government, what was he doing at Navarro's beck and call? Because Marincite Corp. *is* Marincite City. Not sharp, Mayla, she told herself, she was not sharp at all.

She couldn't very well leave Saad to chase their baggage, so the three of them all stood waiting for it to rumble up from the depths of the port. Saad was quiet, was it awkward for him to be standing here? He would say something about her house. Everybody always did. She waited for it. He didn't say anything.

Finally she said, "How's business?"

"Pretty good," he said.

"Have you secured a loan with someone else?"

"Not yet," he said. "You said you'd think about it. Mr. Navarro suggested I talk to you about it before I went to Caribbean Securities."

"I see," she said. If it was true, didn't that mean that Polly Navarro wanted her to make the deal with Saad? She wished she could ask Mr. Navarro, but that would be stupid.

"We don't have to talk about it now," he said. He was uncomfortable.

"MaTE will put me in a conference room, we can talk there."

"It would be better if you came out to the loft," he said.

"No," she said. No. She didn't want to go to the loft. Didn't like it there. People came to her office, she wasn't supposed to go to places like that.

"My partner can't very well come to MaTE," he said.

She almost asked why not. Her mind, where was her mind? If Saad said his partner couldn't come to MaTE he couldn't come. She was going to make a mistake, say or do the wrong thing. She could feel the shakes, creeping around her hands, loosening her stomach. Think this through, she told herself. Why couldn't he come to MaTE? She couldn't think because she was anxious. "He said everything was all right with the Uncles."

"It's okay," Saad said. "The Uncles are no problem."

He wasn't explaining. He looked at the luggage claim rather than at her. She didn't think he was lying but she didn't know. He wasn't going to tell her what was going on.

"Why can't you and I negotiate this?" she asked.

He shook his head. She knew the answer there, she had met his partner, seen how things were between Saad and Moustache.

Dead end. Everything was a dead end and her mind wasn't working. Meet somewhere else? She didn't know places in Marincite, one place was no more safe than another. Tim's duffel rumbled up and he reached between her and Saad to pluck it. It was good to remember Tim was there, big blond Tim.

What to say. What to do. She couldn't very well talk about it now. She had to collect herself, she had to be calm. Take a deep breath, she thought. This anxiety, she thought to herself, it is mindless, it is reaction to stress, you can handle it. Once she had collected herself she could talk to Saad.

"Look," she said, "I need some time to think about this, why don't you call me this evening?"

"I'm sorry," Saad said, "I don't see how that's going to make any difference. The loft is the best place to meet."

"Earlier," she said. "Like about six-thirty."

"I'll call and confirm," he said.

Her hunter-green garment bag rumbled up. "That's mine," she said and Saad leaned to pick it up but Tim said, "I'll get it." Saad took a short step back but Tim just looked at him for moment before bending over and picking up the bag. It was the kind of look Tim had given David when David first came to work for her. Territorial, she thought. Alpha male, squaring off.

Tim, taking care of her. She shouldn't have wanted him to, but Mother of Christ, she did.

Tim didn't like going to see Saad and his partner, and unlike David, he made it clear. He had heard of the part of the city called Cathedral. He said it was a pit, a ghetto, a *budayeen*. He didn't trust Saad Shamsi.

"You liked him well enough when he took us to see jai alai," Mayla pointed out.

Tim didn't bother to answer.

"In and out," she said. "I'll just get a signature on the papers and leave." Polly wanted the loan, then she had to do it.

Tim scowled and hunkered down next to her in the chute. He filled the space in the bubble, overwhelmed it. She had forgotten just what a physical presence Tim could be. Put your arms around me, she thought, I want to hide. Not that she would, it was completely inappropriate and she knew the consequences. His hands looked small compared to the rest of him.

Tim was imposing, if you didn't know him. He would make Saad's partner think twice. He was better than David, that way. Maybe she should remember that when she hired security, hire someone big.

Or maybe she was supposed to hire someone inconspicuous. She didn't know. She didn't know enough about any

of this. The men from the insurance said she had been targeted. Once she was a target, what was she supposed to do?
Get protection? Emigrate? Half the people she went to
school with seemed to have emigrated. Emigrate where,
the U.S.? Follow her mother to Europe? Not to Europe.
She didn't like Europe. When she was fifteen she visited
her mother in Barcelona. She had embarrassed her mother
because she couldn't adapt, couldn't get used to sunlight
and weather. She tried to think of something else. She
wished she could take a pill right now that would make her
think clearly, that would stop her thoughts from skittering
around.

The chute rose into the station, into the light. Cathedral.
The humidity hit her when the chute opened. The refresh
was not as good here as it was in Central and the air was
clammy. Poor man's air.

The loft was empty when they got there. "He's coming,"
Saad said. "He said he'd be here." The loft smelled like
aldehyde, chemical sharp and sweet. "He'll be here," Saad
promised. "You want some coffee? A soft drink?"

"Nothing," she said. She didn't really want coffee or
something to drink, not with that smell.

Tim glowered. Saad looked uncomfortable.

The loft had long tables in it now, and newspapers in
bundled piles in a corner, edges curling in the damp, and a
huge plastic drum with a tube and a siphon. There were
dirty footprints all over, perfect prints of soles with circles,
zigzag lines, and makers' marks, as if the floor had been
mopped and then walked on.

Nobody knew what to say.

"I guess coffee sounds good," Mayla finally said. She
didn't have to drink it but it gave Saad something to do.

Where was Moustache? She didn't like that he wasn't
here. Things weren't going right.

Saad brought coffee for her and Tim. It seemed to her
that it smelled chemical, the same sweet-sharp chemical

she smelled in the air. The surface of the coffee iridesced, like oil, under the light.

Saad went back to get another cup for himself and she heard the door open at the base of the stairs. Moustache came up the steps, followed by the tawny-haired girl, who kept her eyes on the floor. Moustache barely glanced at them. He stomped to the back of the loft and started talking to Saad, speaking low and fast. "What?" Saad said. And again, "What? I can't understand you."

The girl stood in the middle of the loft. She sniffed and rubbed her nose as if she were going to cry.

Moustache struck the table with the flat of his hand. The girl started as if struck. From the way she was standing, Mayla couldn't see her wrist so she didn't know if the girl was wearing a slave bracelet or not.

Saad looked back at them a couple of times, but Moustache talked on and on, words tumbling out, thick with rage. Was he drugged? Mayla thought he had to be. Saad looked back again and Moustache grabbed his shoulder roughly. *"¡ESCHUCHA!"* Then his voice dropped down again, a rumble of consonants that Mayla couldn't decipher.

Maybe she and Tim were supposed to leave? All she wanted was to say to Moustache that she'd give him his damn loan and then she could leave here, and worry about these people later.

The girl shifted her feet a little, as if she would like to sit down.

Moustache looked around and said, "What do you want?"

Mayla looked at the tawny-haired girl. The girl looked at Mayla. And Saad said, placatingly, "About the loan. She is here about the loan."

"Big anglo," Moustache said. "Your boyfriend?"

He was talking to her, not the tawny-haired girl at all. "No," Mayla said, her voice rising in surprise. "No, he's not my boyfriend." Did Tim act like her boyfriend? She hadn't even thought Moustache noticed them there.

"Who is he?"

"Her security," Saad said.

"I thought her security is the little rat-faced *chino.*"

"He doesn't work for me anymore," Mayla said.

Moustache didn't like that answer. He scowled at her. *"Chinga,"* he said.

Tim scowled back. Don't, she thought, don't start anything. It doesn't matter.

"What is your problem!" Moustache shouted at her. He strode across the room, into her face, so close she took a step back. "You play mindgames with us, what? WHAT IS YOUR PROBLEM, BITCH!" He was standing so close that spittle flicked her face and his breath had a strange odor—almost fruity like aftershave—and the whites of his eyes looked yellow. She flinched, and he grabbed her arm. She pulled away and Tim grabbed for Moustache.

Moustache jerked away and the tawny-haired girl shrieked.

"Hey hey hey," Saad said. "Easy. Everything is all right."

"Don't touch her," Tim said. "You hear me? Don't touch her."

"You think you own everything? This is Marincite," Moustache said, ignoring Tim, "you are in my city now. Here, I could have you both disappear. No one would find you. Anglos, no one here likes anglos. No one likes an anglo *chinga.* No one would care. Here, this is not the capital, this is Marincite."

"Hey," Saad said, his voice smooth and placating, "nobody is talking about disappearing. We are going to make a loan, that's all."

"Shut up," Moustache said, not even looking at Saad. "Listen, I just want you to understand the rules. We are not impressed by *las norteamericanas* here. Your big country may be rich, but it's far away. So don't play mindgames anymore."

She wasn't North American. She knew better than to correct him, don't explain, it would only make him angry if she explained. But she wasn't from the U.S., white skin or no white skin, she was Caribbean. He was crazy, he was toxic. What did it matter what he said? The tawny-haired girl was watching, watching. Not moving at all, even her breath invisible.

He was looking at Tim, and then he started to grin. The tawny-haired girl covered her mouth with her hand. *Madre de Diós,* Mayla thought. The tawny-haired girl looked scared and that was bad. This is bad, Mayla thought, the words in her head. He's going to hurt Tim.

Tim didn't look scared, Tim looked furious. "What's funny?" he asked.

"Tim—"

"Estúpido," Moustache said, grinning. Behind him, Saad looked scared, too.

"What is your problem?" Tim asked.

Moustache turned around and walked away a few steps. Turned around again and he had a gun. A little gun, the size of his hand, all graphite gray. Not like the handgun that Tim carried under the seat of the car. Small. Illegal-looking.

Nobody said anything. Please God, Mayla thought, let it be all right. Just let this be over. In a couple of hours this will be over.

Moustache was full of contained energy. He was looking at Tim and she knew not to move because if she moved he might look at her and she didn't want Moustache to think about her. It was awful, hoping that he wouldn't notice her, being glad that Tim was his target. It was sinful. But she did, she couldn't help it. Don't notice me, she thought. Don't move, she thought to Tim.

Tim did not move. Like the tawny-haired girl, he did not even seem to breathe.

"Bueno," Moustache said. Then he looked at her and she felt her breath stop, a pain in her chest. His eyes were brown, the whites yellowed; his eyes were diseased looking and he was watching her with his rancid eyes. She didn't know what was going to happen.

He aimed the gun at her and she could not imagine what she should do. Move, leap away like the vid. But the truth was she couldn't think. If she moved he would shoot her. Maybe if she didn't move, he would not shoot. But if he was going to shoot she should move. She could not think, could not make herself move. How would she know when he was going to shoot? How would she know when to jump? Please, God, don't let him shoot. She was afraid of the pain. She was afraid to die. She couldn't. She couldn't. Please.

Nobody did anything.

She could not even look at the gun, just his rancid eyes. The way the irises looked as if they were not sharply round, as if the edges were breaking down, melted looking.

It went on and on. How long had she stood here like this? A minute, five minutes? Ten minutes? She had to do something. She wanted to just be still, hope it went away. She had to do something. Breathe. The veins in his yellowed eyes. Maybe he had a medical condition? Jaundice? People didn't get jaundice anymore, did they?

She opened her mouth, but nothing happened.

Be still. Don't startle him, if she startled him he'd jerk, he'd squeeze, he'd fire.

"Hey," she said, so softly, because that was how her voice came.

He didn't jerk, didn't move at all. Now he was going to kill her.

"Oye, eschucha," she said. "Hey, listen."

He didn't answer her. She would make him angry. Just a little push and he would shoot.

"Hey," she said. "We're here to make you a loan. We're here to do a little business."

Moustache watched her with his yellow eyes.

"Everybody is here to do business," Saad echoed. His voice sounded smooth, soothing. His voice made her hopeful. His voice said everything would be all right. But maybe that wasn't true. Some times when you thought everything was going to be all right, it wasn't.

"We want to talk," she said.

And Moustache turned and aimed the gun into the office. The gunshot was a little sound, just a blurt.

The tawny-haired girl shrieked and Tim started. Moustache laughed. "No mindgames," Moustache said. "You see? No mindgames."

Mayla was suddenly aware of the sweet chemical smell again, so strong she felt dizzy. "No mindgames," she agreed. She would go through the motions, she would say anything he wanted, and then she would get away.

Moustache looked around the loft. Looked at Saad and grinned. They were all standing around watching him, waiting for what he would do. Mayla could feel the individual tickles of perspiration on her ribs. Her jacket would be perspiration stained, maybe ruined.

"Maybe," Moustache said, "we should show the lady what we make?"

"I don't think that's a good idea," Saad said, soft.

"Fuck you," Moustache said conversationally. That struck him as funny. "Fuck you," he said again, liking the sound of it. "I think we should."

Humor him, diffuse the situation. "Okay," Mayla said.

Saad looked startled. Moustache rounded on her, delighted. "You see? *La norteamericana* wants to see."

"I don't think—" Saad said.

"That's right," Moustache said, "you don't think. Go get some bracelets."

Saad went back into the office. Mayla found she didn't want him out of sight, she felt better when he was right there. He could talk to Moustache. Tim was just watching, very still, his face blank. She didn't know what he was thinking, or what he was planning. Don't do anything, she thought, just don't be crazy.

She heard the jingle of keys, loud in the loft. Moustache was looking at her, and he still had the gun in his hand, although it wasn't aimed at her. It wasn't aimed at anyone, as if he had just forgotten it. She tried not to look at it, so she wouldn't remind him he had it, but she didn't know what to look at. Should she look at Moustache? She couldn't look away, she needed to watch him, she had to know what he was doing. He could do anything.

If she kept looking at him, would he get mad? She couldn't look at his eyes, so she glanced away, but looked back at him, in his eyes. Away, across the loft, at Tim. Back at Moustache, back down at the gun, back up at his strange eyes. She didn't know what to do with her gaze.

Saad came back out of the office and she could look at him. Then she could watch Moustache again because *he* was watching Saad.

"Let's see," Moustache said.

Slave bracelets. They didn't look like anything, just a plate of dull metal on a strap like a watchband. He had six or seven of them and he held them out to Moustache, who selected one and held it up, dangling it like the strap was a tail.

"You try one before?" he asked.

"No," Mayla said.

"Go ahead. I think you like it."

"That's okay," she said.

"No, really," Moustache said. "It's good. You try."

"I," she swallowed, "I can't."

"Are you playing games?" he said, conversational, and she felt the prickle on her neck.

"Let me look at it," she temporized. She held out her hand to take it but Moustache took her hand and turned it over. Tim gave a little start.

"Enough," he said.

"Shut up," Mayla said, sharply. That startled him.

Moustache laughed and the color started in Tim's neck. Be embarrassed, she thought, just don't be stupid.

Moustache's hand was damp. Like the air. She wanted to wipe her hand off. He held her hand a moment, as if he was going to tell her fortune, looking at her palm, at her long fingers. Maybe he was, maybe he was making her future. She thought, she would be changed by this, by the slave bracelet. Like losing her virginity.

Moustache turned her hand back over and put the bracelet on so that the flat metal plate was against the pale inside of her wrist. Then he did the flat catch.

She expected a jolt, like an electric current, but it wasn't like that at all. No spike, no high. But her head felt clear. Her thoughts weren't all skittering. She felt calmer. Still scared, but calmer.

"See? Is not so bad." Moustache smiled at her.

And well. Not tired, when was the last time she had not felt tired? She realized that people felt tired all the time. The only time people didn't feel tired was when they were really angry, or really happy, or really frightened, and then they couldn't appreciate it. Now she could feel what it was like not to be tired. It was wonderful, as if something had been lifted off her. This was the way people were supposed to feel.

"She likes it," Moustache said.

She did like it. Very much, she liked it.

"Now we will discuss business?" Moustache said.

"Okay," she said.

Tim shook his head.

"It's not like that," she said. "It doesn't make your head muddled." It made it easier to think, because her mind wasn't dragged down by all those feelings and tiredness. She felt good.

She could weigh the pros and cons. She dug out her papers and her chips. Her hands were shaking a little. She was still afraid; if she thought about it she could find it, her fear. It was a thing in her thoughts, like a rock in a river, and she could flow around it. Because of the bracelet. Good to be afraid, just not so afraid that she couldn't act.

Maybe she couldn't trust her thoughts? Bracelets were illegal. She laid out her papers and Moustache started reading. But they were illegal because of the degeneration they caused in the nervous system. Because of prolonged use. And they were addicting because they really did enhance. So she should take advantage of this one time. Lucky, because this was the one time she really needed it.

While Moustache read she looked around the loft. People were amazing. Tim was amazing. His skin was amazing, flushed with capillaries in his face and neck, so smooth over his forehead. Tim was so handsome. But so was Saad, with his high temples and his beautiful, neat hands. Dark and almost manicured looking. People were extraordinary, and nobody realized it except maybe for a few great artists and poets. How completely artificial it was to divide people into beautiful and ugly.

Moustache handed each paper to Saad as soon as he had read it. Mayla looked at the tawny-haired girl. She was strained and tired looking, but beautiful, too. Youth was truly astounding. No wonder they all worshiped youth. Even through her tiredness she glowed, and Mayla felt the pang of loss. And she never knew it was hers to lose because she never realized she had it until she looked in the mirror one morning when she got out of the shower and saw the skin of her collarbones and neck and realized she was thirty years old and it was gone. It wasn't fair.

Moustache signed, Saad signed. She took the papers. "That's it," she said.

"So when do we get the money?" Saad said.

"It'll take a couple of days to process, it has to go through the credit committee for approval," she said. "I'm not in Julia, so maybe four days, and then it'll be in your account."

"All record keeping comes through me," Saad said.

All record keeping was by numbered account, no names. "Your PO," she said.

"Perhaps you would like to buy a bracelet," Moustache said. Pleased with himself.

She could not. She fingered it, not wanting to take it off. That was why it was addicting, because it just made people more human, more themselves. Enhanced them.

The tawny-haired girl smiled. *"Hermana,"* she said. "Sister." A smile like Moustache's, pleased with itself, and Mayla wondered if she had misunderstood. Was the girl Moustache's daughter?

Mayla unbuckled the clasp and the weight of twenty-one atmospheres fell on her like an ache. She shuddered. For a moment she didn't want to move. The tiredness swallowed her up. Every day she felt this way, for the rest of her life, she felt this way. Oh, God, she couldn't bear it.

"If you want to buy," Moustache said, "you let us know."

"Let's go," Tim said.

And Saad, what did Saad think? Had he ever tried it? Could he see that she was hooked? She handed the bracelet to Moustache. She wanted it back. Moustache looked at her with his yellow eyes and she thought for a moment, now that he had what he wanted he would kill them.

But the loan wasn't through committee yet.

Her mind started to go in different directions. She thought of the house, of hiring security, of the fact that now she was bound to Moustache by this loan.

"Come on," Tim said, urgent. Tim was scared.

Oh, God, she was so tired and so scared and so unhappy. She gathered up her papers.

"Be in touch," Moustache said. "We can do business again."

He was crazy. She had bound herself to a married man, married to him by the bank and Polly Navarro. She didn't know what to do. She couldn't think at all, could do nothing through her misery except follow Tim down the hollow steps, her heels clicking on the empty steps as if they were drums, all the sound bouncing.

"What the hell did you do that for?" Tim said on the street.

"What?" she said.

"Try the thing on? It could have done anything, you didn't know if it was wired right or not! It could have fried your nervous system!"

"It didn't," she said.

"Are you sure?" he asked. He grabbed her wrist and started down the street.

She wanted to run away. She wanted to go somewhere where she didn't have to act, didn't have to think. "After neural stimulation, there's a bottoming," she said.

"What?"

She was mumbling. Louder, she said, "After neural stimulation, people bottom out. I've read about it."

"Great," Tim said.

She didn't want to see Saad Shamsi ever again. She most certainly didn't want to see Moustache.

She wouldn't put the papers through. She'd burn them. It was illegal, a signed contract was a binding document and destruction of it without the other party's consent was against the law. But what were they going to do, take her to court? She didn't care about the Marincite loan, it wasn't worth dying for. If she got the Marincite loan then she might eventually get promoted and then things would get even more complicated.

She wanted to go somewhere and live, maybe Del Sud. Buy a flat, live by herself, watch the vid. Have a simple life. Quit the world. Anything was better than her life now.

She sat in a conference room, waiting to talk to Polly Navarro about the Marincite loan, about the takeover target to finance MaTE's independence. She had a list of likely candidates. The air in this room was clean and dry. The window looked down on Manhattan. As far as she could tell, it was modern Manhattan. She had lived in Manhattan, she probably should have known whether it was a modern view or not.

The hard light reflected off the wood conference table. She didn't know if she should tell Polly that she wasn't going to make Saad's loan or not. She knew she'd have to find a way to let him know, but she didn't know if she was supposed to pretend that Polly didn't know what the company was or not. She knew she wasn't supposed to tell him.

Whatever happened, she had to think about being a banker.

She was either going to have to deal with people like Moustache and Anna Eminike or emigrate. Or just wait for something to happen. And she couldn't deal with Moustache or Anna Eminike, they were not people one dealt with.

Emigrate.

At one time in her life she had wanted to leave Caribe. More than anything. When she was fifteen she had finally gone to the surface for the first time when she went to Barcelona to see her mother.

When she was fifteen, she thought she was maybe the only person at her school who had never been to the surface. It couldn't have been true, but she remembered it seemed that way.

As a girl she thought that she was really a surface person. She knew she would love weather. Wind; wind would be exciting, wind was like *Wuthering Heights,* she couldn't exactly explain how but it was. And once she got there she would be with her mother.

The sub was boring, Miami was strange. She had done five days of decompression in decomp at Port Authority and she was reacting to the change. It was night, but the lights in the terminal were too bright, the lights on poles outside even brighter. And the air smelled funny, organic: like food and garbage; potato and carrot scrapings. Plants. Grass. Nobody had ever told her that the surface smelled funny—even the ocean was loud and over the familiar briny smell it stank.

She landed in Barcelona jangled and tired. Her mother was waiting with Gabriel, her four-year-old half-brother, and her mother's second husband, Tito. Her mother's hair was blonde instead of brown and she spoke lisping Spanish to the four-year-old and the husband. Mayla understood a little Spanish, but not very much.

The sunlight was too bright, her head ached and her eyes watered. Barcelona was loud. They got on a tram and her half-brother stared at her with round black eyes, and her mother's husband smiled too much. She couldn't think of what to say. Every time she looked at her mother who was silhouetted against one of the blinding windows, she got afterimages when she turned away. The husband got off before they got home, he had to go to work. He worked in one of the blinding glass towers, unnervingly high. There was too much space, the sky was so blue, it seemed impossible that any stretch of space would be such an obvious, unnatural color.

She was afraid she'd get a sunburn. Food tasted strange, salt wasn't as salty and everything had a funny, metallic taste. It's just adjustment, her mother said. At dinner, her mother kept speaking in Spanish to Tito and Gabriel. Tito tried to talk to her, but she didn't understand him, even when he said things she knew the Spanish words for.

"Mayla," her mother said, "I wanted to bring you here for so long, but Jimmy's mother—" her mother pursed her lips. Her mother wasn't going to talk about Gram. Mayla didn't talk about Gram either, but it made conversation oddly disjointed. Her mother kept saying, "Tell me about your life." But after she had talked about school, Gram was in everything.

Her mother took her shopping, bought her expensive things, with collars of eyelet lace, a sleeveless silk top, a quilted jacket. She tried to play with her half-brother, but he made her nervous. He liked to be tickled and he liked to wrestle, but pretty quickly he got rough, hitting her leg with his fist and laughing, and she didn't know how to make him stop.

The third day she was there they went downtown again and shopped. They were on the bus coming back from the city, and for the first time since she had arrived, she felt as if she could look out at the street without her eyes watering. "It's cloudy," her mother said. "You don't need your sunglasses, Mayla."

But she liked them. "I can see better," she said.

There were trees and they pulled in the wind. It was like the vid, watching the trees. Mayla felt as if she wanted to be outside in the wind. She felt afraid, but it was a good kind of afraid—excited. Water started dripping down from the roof of the bus, condensation maybe, streaking her window. Streaking all the windows. Darkening the street. It wasn't from the bus, she thought, it was rain.

"Oh no," her mother said, "I don't have an umbrella. We'll have to run." Her mother leaned forward and put her hand against the window. She looked excited. When they got to their stop, her mother took her hand, and pulled her down the steps, out into the rain, running.

The rain was pounding down, and just as they jumped to the ground there was a crack, like an explosion and she started because an explosion at home meant the sea was coming in, an explosion at home meant you were dead. Her mother pulled her, running. Mayla's face was wet and she was afraid to breathe in; the air was full of water, it was unnatural, it was cold and awful, she couldn't breathe, she felt that if she took a breath she would drown. Her mother dragged her, and she saw white sparks, things around her got black until she could only see what was in front of her. Her mother kept pulling and pulling, until they were under the overhang at her mother's house. She heard herself gasp and instead of just breathing she was crying in great, shaking sobs.

"Oh baby," her mother said, "You'll be all right. I'm

sorry baby, I'm sorry." Her mother wanted her to stop crying, she could tell, but she was scared and she hated this place. It hurt her mother, her crying, but she didn't care, she didn't care at all, and she kept right on.

That was when she knew that she wasn't a surface person.

She looked back over her list. Owen, Tumipamba's successor at MaTE, got there before Polly. Of course, Polly would be late. He was the CFO, he could be as late as he wanted.

"What have you got?" Owen asked, and she passed the list over to him.

She watched him read. Owen was from the U.S., Pennsylvania or something. She wished she'd been born in the U.S., then she wouldn't have to worry about adapting.

Owen was still reading when Polly walked in. "Morning Mayla, how's it going?"

"Okay," she said. "Oh, Polly, about that clinic loan, there's been some problems." Her heart was beating hard.

"What's wrong?" Polly seemed genuine, not accusative. As if it didn't matter to him.

"There's a rider on the loan, with a partner. Normally I wouldn't have any trouble, you know . . ." she faltered.

Polly nodded.

"The partner. I can't work with the partner," she said. "Nobody could work with the partner."

"Oh," Polly said, "I'm sorry to hear that. I'd hoped it would give First Hawaiian a little presence. But it's really pretty small anyway."

"Yeah," she said. "I mean, I'd have liked the business, for, you know, presence, like you said." She took a deep breath. "But I can't. The partner . . . is a problem. I can't get around it. I can't do the loan."

"Right," he said. "Well, if anything else comes up, I'll try to steer it your way."

It sounded all right. Even though Polly had sent Saad to meet her at the subport. Maybe Polly really didn't care about the loan, maybe he didn't even know about Saad's partner. Maybe he really had been trying to do her a favor.

Maybe it was all right. Maybe she really could still make the right banking decisions.

She wanted to escape. She wanted to go to Del Sud, get a flat, a pretty little flat, and live an orderly existence. Find a different world, a simpler place. Any world was better than this.

9

Virtual Weather

oldiers came right down the street," Santos said. "My grandmother told my mama to buy rice so we bought twenty-five kilos of rice. And water, we bought a lot of water. You couldn't buy air. But it wasn't the same as a war. It wasn't the same because there was only one side. There was the soldiers and there was just people. And it was in the city, not on a real battlefield." Santos was talking about the Liberation.

They were hunkered down in the high grass, watching for the other team. This time they were on patrol, waiting for an unnaturally accelerated twilight and darkness.

"You weren't born when it happened," David said.

"Yeah, but I heard about it." Santos' pirate face was old enough to remember the Liberation. "I know it wasn't like war."

"Sometimes war is in cities," David pointed out mildly.

"You can't have a real war in a city like Julia, there's not enough space. You know, no tanks, no planes," Santos sounded nostalgic. Was nostalgia the right way to describe it? Nostalgia for a reality built from vids and films.

The sky had just started to darken. Around them stood yellow grass, waving a bit in the wind. It should have been scratchy and smelled like sweet straw but he couldn't even smell the helmet anymore. David put his hand out and felt a tickle across the palm of the glove that was not quite like reality.

Santos didn't know it was not quite like grass because Santos had never been in real grass. Just like Santos didn't know that all that had to happen for something to qualify as a war was for events to total a certain quantity of anarchy and death.

It would be maybe ten minutes until darkness. He hated to wait, he didn't like maneuvers in the dark. He was wasting money, sitting here in virtual grass, waiting to do something he wasn't going to enjoy. If he'd known they were going to be doing a run in the dark he would have begged off.

Something chirped in the grass. The sky was blackening perceptibly. They would start moving before it got dark, as soon as it got gray enough to blur the edges of things. Maybe he could get killed quick. "Santos," he said, "when you are shot, is there a loud noise?"

"Yes?" Santos said, not understanding.

"When the bomb was dropped on me, there was a loud noise. When I get killed, last time. If you are shot and killed, there is this noise?"

"Sometimes," Santos said.

Shit. Well, maybe after this he wouldn't play anymore, it wasn't worth it. Spending money to do something he didn't like, that was stupid.

There was a crack of lightning and he jumped.

"Fuck," Santos said.

The twilight was plum colored, but David didn't know how much of that was storm. He hadn't known it was part of the scenario. "What is it?" he asked.

"Thunderstorm," Santos said.

"I *know* it is a thunderstorm. Did we pick a thunderstorm?" He couldn't imagine why.

"No," Santos said. "Sometimes the program just does it. You know, weather."

If he had wanted weather, David thought, he would not be playing virtual wargames.

"I like it when it rains," Santos said. "It's more real." Santos had never been in the rain.

The rain came towards them. He could just see it as a darker curtain in the plum-colored darkness. It was like watching a vid, there was no heavy pre-storm calm, no shock wave of cold air riding before the rain, no pregnant scent of weather on the wind. He couldn't smell anything. He could feel the handlebars, feel the treadmill he was sitting on. And then it washed across them and the sound of rain was all around them and he could see nothing at all.

In the blackness he closed his eyes and concentrated on the treadmill, on the weight of the helmet on his cheeks and across the bridge of his nose. His hairnet was messed up by the strap around the back of his head. He was sitting on a treadmill in a cubicle, listening to the rain drum all around him while he himself remained curiously dry. The shapes on his eyelids were green at first, then red Rorschach blots, random retinal firings.

He could pull off the helmet. He could quit. He could get up off the treadmill and walk away. Meph was waiting in the room. David would find a job, waiting tables, unloading skids, something. Earn a little money instead of spending it, like a teenaged boy, on pseudo-experience. Santos had never seen anything but a virtual construct called Lezard, and if they met on the street, Santos wouldn't know him and he wouldn't know Santos. "He purged," Santos would say, "we were just sitting there and he just cleared the tanks, you know? Gone. Nothing. Me and the fucking rain."

He felt Santos' hand close around his wrist and his glove

pulled slightly. "It'll give us cover!" Santos shouted in his ear.

The treadmill jerked and shuddered. It was a little like walking on slick ground, but not much. The ground wouldn't really have been wet yet anyway. He couldn't see. They could walk right through the enemy's camp and not even know it in the darkness. This was foolish. They couldn't even use the mine sweep to watch for mines, they couldn't read it in this rain. Did they even have mines in this game? Well, they had the sweep, and mines scared him to death, so he supposed they did.

Lightning, and the landscape flashed around them, overexposed. It was gone before he got a sense of anything and the thunder was a painful crack that jolted him so much he went to his knees. The treadmill stopped for a moment and he heard, below the sound of the rain, his own ragged breathing.

Santos pulled on his hand, a phantom tug without real weight behind it. "Come *on*."

Fuck. He got to his feet carefully, not trusting the treadmill. Night goggles. Why didn't they have night goggles? In real fighting everybody used them. But at least the rain seemed to be slowing down, it was less noisy although he still couldn't see anything. Nothing made sense, they should have been waiting for the rain to stop. They couldn't see anything, they were stupid to be moving in weather like this. If they had been moving against a real enemy, that enemy would have been on his home ground and they would be blundering around in the rain and dark. He thought he could make out shapes, a bluff to his left, or maybe a big piece of equipment. He strained to make out the shape, maybe the turret of a tank? He should be able to see the gun—

Lightning again and the left fell away down a gentle slope, no bluff, no tank, but farther away black hump-shapes hunched in the rain—

He crouched and pulled on Santos' hand. He thought

the shapes were tents, tents or vehicles. "What?" Santos said. The rain was less, Santos didn't have to shout.

"Wait," David hissed.

They waited for the lightning. He wanted to quit, he wanted to go home. How long had he been here? Not more than thirty minutes, that meant they had better than an hour, maybe ninety minutes left. The darkness was making him crazy and he was getting a headache. Had someone from the tents/trucks seen them outlined in the lightning? He was pretty sure it was a camp. If it was, Santos would alert the rest of the group with a remote and then would they sit in the dark and wait? This was not like real weather at all. If it were like real weather then there would have been more lightning by now.

His knees were aching so he eased into a sitting position. (It was hard to shake the feeling that he was going to sit on wet ground, but the treadmill was reassuringly dry.) If the enemy had seen them, they'd probably be crawling towards them now, coming up the slight rise. No lightning. Was the program monitoring? Maybe they weren't getting lightning because they needed it? Maybe the weather programming was particularly sadistic?

The sound of rain was less. It was much harder to keep track of virtual rain than of real rain. Santos sighed next to him and he wanted to shush him. If the enemy was crawling towards them they might hear.

Kill me, he thought, kill me and get it over with. Santos didn't know that fighting a war consisted of long periods of anxious boredom punctuated by intense short periods of terror.

The rain, if it was still raining, was down to a fine mist. Now what were they supposed to do? It was still too dark to see, and now they wouldn't even get lightning. And for all he knew, around them was enemy.

The sky grayed a bit, suddenly faintly luminescent. Dawn? Already? There was the feeling of movement in the sky, of wind. Then he saw edges, illuminated pale, and the clouds seemed to tear. The moon shown through a rip in the clouds, bright and defined—not dawn but moonrise— and then disappeared. Then the tatters of cloud cleared the moon again and he could see an empty landscape that seemed positively flooded with light. Below them the black shapes of enemy tents, but no soldiers around them.

His shoulders were aching with tension. Santos fumbled with the remote and David saw it blink red before Santos set it face down in the grass. Just a tiny thing, a little smaller than the palm of his hand.

Santos leaned over so he was close to David's ear. "Let's take them."

"Shouldn't we wait?" David whispered back.

"Nah," Santos said, pointing at the camp with his chin, "most of them will be NPC." NPC: Non-Player-Characters. Great; even if they were fake people on automatic pilot they still outnumbered David and Santos.

Santos slung his rifle around and David felt his irritation rising. Stupid kid, always in a hurry, not thinking. He had half a mind to let Santos go running in alone, get himself killed if he wanted to.

It was a game, he told himself. They had been playing for almost half an hour without any combat. The point of this was to "go in." He sighed, and reached back and tapped his shoulder so his weightless rifle would swing around. Once he had it in his hands it at least felt solid. No heft, just the solid feel of it. Maybe if they played some sort of space game then the weightlessness wouldn't matter.

In an hour and a half this would all be over. He could go home. Next time he would check whether the maneuvers were in daylight or at night and if they said night he'd claim he was busy.

He was a grown man. This was a game. He could separate reality from game. He should be fair to Santos, let him have his fun.

"Okay," he said.

"Ready?" Santos said.

Not exactly, but he nodded.

Santos ran half-crouched towards the tents. Best would have been to wiggle through the grass, but that would have been stupid on a treadmill. David blindly grabbed the handlebar and tried to follow. He couldn't run crouched the way Santos had because all this sitting and kneeling and falling had his knee aching, but he hunched.

Santos lobbed a grenade and as the grenade launched through the air someone opened fire from the camp, a sharp ta-ta-ta-ta-ta-tat. David checked, cringing, waiting for something, and then made himself run. He was running heavily, he could feel his feet thumping on the treadmill. No element of surprise. Of course, the people in this camp had been sitting around in a thunderstorm for half an hour, waiting to be attacked.

The lights went on, the grenade exploded, and Santos lobbed another one. David tapped his belt and then he had one. (The hardest part of this whole game was remembering the gestures that accessed his weapons.) He tapped the pin and lobbed it, grateful that he had the sense to activate it before throwing it. It was true, an overhand throw from training years ago that he didn't know his arm remembered until he'd done it. The concussions were slightly staggering, but very satisfying.

Soldiers came boiling out of tents. A woman soldier with a long tail of swinging hair came out of one tent, crackling faintly with a blue glow like St. Elmo's fire. Some strange weapon from the game? A program glitch? He checked again, looked at Santos. Santos had seen her and turned his fire on her. "A PC!" he shouted.

David was firing, and she was firing back at them. The air was full of noise and he wanted to fall but he was on the treadmill, so he was looking for cover, ducking behind tents as if canvas would protect him. The soldiers were all around, the NPCs, the program-generated people, they were like chaff. He aimed and sprayed, blindly firing and the three in front of him jerked and fell. So easy, he thought, not like people at all. They ran and shot and pointed and shouted but seemed ineffective. He aimed at one of them and squeezed the trigger (the trigger was a little soft on this thing) and the soldier fell, shots stitched in a seam across his chest. He ducked behind another tent, always moving, always keeping himself from being too much of a target.

The woman crackling with faint blue fire (no brighter than a gas flame in sunlight) she seemed immune to their shooting. Maybe the blue was some sort of protection? Santos kept trained on her, so David worked on her too, ducking, firing, ducking. She turned and ran, evidently not trusting her own equipment and David kept trained on her, a steady stream of bullets, there was still firing around him but he ignored it, keeping his gun on the woman, it should have been heating up, he should have at least emptied the clip by now but it kept on firing, die, you goddamn bitch—

Something huge lurched to his right, but it wasn't anything, he had lost part of his view, he could only see out of his left eye. Stupid goddamn moment for the helmet to screw up. Cheap equipment. No maintenance. He fired, the world suddenly flatter. He couldn't focus out of his left eye as well. The woman turned to fire, pausing, and he and Santos trained on her. She went down, finally, and he felt the rising surge of triumph, and the blue flickered all around her like lightning and was gone.

Santos whooped, adrenaline joy.

The rest were running, easily cut down. And then the little camp was in tatters. Bodies everywhere. It was an astounding amount of destruction for two people. Animated violence. "Great job," Santos said, standing there, looking around. "We got to get out of here, they have reinforcements coming, you know?"

Only seeing out of one eye was really annoying. He could hear out of both ears, all right. Maybe he should exit the game and see if he could get another cube? But how would he get back in the game?

"We should go that way, I think," Santos pointed and glanced back to confirm. "Oh shit, Lezard."

"What?" David said.

"Why didn't you tell me you were wounded?"

"I am?" David said. Of course, he was penalized.

"Can you see?"

"With one eye."

"Cristo," Santos said, "you have a medikit?"

A medikit? It had never even dawned on him that they would use a medikit in virtual. "No, I don't think so."

"I got one, wait—" Santos fumbled a moment, tapped his pocket, didn't like what came up and fumbled some more. Then he had a blue kit box in his hand. He peered at the cover in the moonlight. "Yeah, it's still all right."

He opened the box but the gloves didn't allow fine manipulation so he took out a packet and waved it in David's face. The packet disappeared—used up, David assumed. "Okay," Santos said, "now you won't bleed to death or die of infection."

Die of infection? In an hour and a half? Virtual infections, like virtual weather, must be accelerated.

"I want to check the tents," Santos said. "Only for a minute."

He still couldn't see anything out of his right eye. Seeing out of only his left eye was strange. He looked around, trying to focus, found himself looking at a corpse. Well, there were a lot of them.

The man lay flopped on his back, his chest, abdomen and groin bloody but not ruined. His blood was black and wet in the moonlight and his fatigues looked genuinely soaked (David thought if he touched the body his fingers would come away black) but it was curiously cosmetic. He was flopped there convincingly enough, abandoned the way corpses look, but he looked bland. Features too regular, somehow. Not particularly handsome. He had an in-